MW00584531

Praise for *Zero Saints*

"Call him the Barrio Palahniuk, a badass Henry Miller, Charles Willeford in Cholo-land—whatever the moniker, for my money Gabino Iglesias is one of the most fearless, original and riveting writers working today. If there's any justice on this hellhole of a planet, *Zero Saints*—an instant, wild-ass classic—should launch its author far from outlier status into the wet, palpitating heart of contemporary literature. This is a fierce, nasty, beautiful, sucker-punch of a novel. You'd be an idiot not to read it immediately."

— Jerry Stahl, author of
Permanent Midnight and *I, Fatty*

"Zero Saints is a damn miracle. Gabino Iglesias' knockout novel manages to merge cinematic crime thrills—recalling the best of Thompson, Himes, and Lynch—with a scathing portrait of the psychogeographical effects of life along la frontera. Relentless in both its down-and-dirty action and emotional truth, Zero Saints is a work of menace and magic and a beautiful prayer for our damaged souls."

— Jeremy Robert Johnson, author of
Skullcrack City and *Entropy in Bloom*

"This is as good as it gets...a bad ass shot of the finest literary mezcal....and one damned intense, hellraising tale served up by a writer in full control of the throttle. Iglesias brilliantly guides us on a hurtling, breathtaking tour of Austin's underbelly -- and firmly cements his stature in the top ranks of the most original noir novelists at work today. In a watered down world, *Zero Saints* is the real thing -- a scary, howlingly funny, painfully aching window into that darkly savage world north of the Mexican border."

— Bill Minutaglio, author of
Dallas 1963 and *In Search of the Blues*

"Iglesias is a master of compact phrasing and perfectly paced suspense."

— *Los Angeles Review of Books*

"Like shoveling into buried cable, there is eye-popping electricity in these pages, hand-clenching power in Iglesias' words. You crack the spine and there's no letting go. *Zero Saints* is 14,000-volt barrio noir."

— David Joy, author of *The Line that Held Us*

"*Zero Saints* is a fun book, expanding the confines of its genre. It is also necessary and smart."

— *El Paso Times*

"A wonderful melding of horror, crime, and noir."

— Brian Keene, author of *The Rising*

"*Zero Saints* filled with such shimmering scenes, scenes that blend the ordinary and the weird, the sacred and the profane, violence with poetry, gore that manages to gouge its way onto your heart even as the horror gnaws at your soul."

— *This Is Horror*

"An original, violent, oddly beautiful, bat-shit-crazy mix of crime and horror."

— Paul Tremblay, author of *The Cabin at the End of the World*

"*Zero Saints* is straightforward, hardcore noir fiction, sometimes brutally violent, fast paced, and brooding. It's also brutally honest at times and looks issues like poverty and immigration right in the face boldly and fearlessly."

— *Shotgun Logic*

"Iglesias writes like a dream, balancing the strange and the surreal with the criminal elements superbly."

— *Lovecraft eZine*

A Broken River Books Original
Broken River Books
12205 Elkhorn Ct.
El Paso, TX 79936

Copyright © 2018 by Gabino Iglesias

Cover art and design copyright © 2018 by Matthew Revert
www.matthewrevert.com

Interior design by J David Osborne

All rights reserved. No part of this book may be repro-
duced or transmitted in any form or by any means, elec-
tronic or mechanical, including photocopying, recording,
or by any information storage and retrieval system, without the written consent of the publisher, except where per-
mitted by law.

This is a work of fiction. All names, characters, places,
and incidents are the product of the author's imagination.
Where the names of actual celebrities or corporate entities
appear, they are used for fictional purposes and do not con-
stitute assertions of fact. Any resemblance to real events or
persons, living or dead, is coincidental.

ISBN: 978-1-940885-49-0

Printed in the USA.

COYOTE SONGS

a barrio noir

by
Gabino Iglesias

BROKEN RIVER BOOKS

EL PASO, TX

for

J David Osborne and Ben Whitmer

PEDRITO

Pedrito sat in the back of the truck and watched his father pull the front half of a buffalo carp from their cooler, place it on top of a plastic tarp, and chop off a chunk of it with a large knife. The pink flesh shook like jelly. The smell of dead fish and congealing blood crept up Pedrito's nose. Most people disliked the odor, but for the boy, the smell of putrefying fish meat meant being outside and spending time with his father, so he loved it even if it stuck to his clothes all day and made his mother shout at him to take a bath as soon as they walked in the door.

Pedrito's father chopped a second chunk of fish off and placed both pieces next to each other on top of the tarp. He dropped the fish's head to the ground and kicked it away from their truck with a dusty boot and wiped his hands on his jeans, which were so dirty they looked like camo pants.

Don Pedro, Pedrito's father, reached over a few fishing implements that were scattered in the back of the truck and pulled a tackle box toward him. He unsnapped the two latches in the front and opened it. The three pieces of plastic that held his fishing gear transformed into a small staircase to nowhere. Plastic fish with feathers tied to their undersides, colorful worms that looked like candy, and fishing hooks of various sizes shone under the unrelenting sun. Don Pedro's calloused hands rummaged through the gear as if he'd trained the hooks to never bite. Pedrito kept his eyes glued to his father. He knew that every part of the process was important, and if his father was quiet, that meant he had to watch carefully to internalize everything. He knew internalizing was important because his teacher said so at the end of every class. And she was right. Some of his father's most important lessons, the boy had learned, were given in complete silence.

Don Pedro kept digging around in the tackle box for a few seconds before pulling out a black treble hook. It looked like a tiny, lightless chandelier. He grabbed one of the chunks of buffalo with his left hand and deftly pierced it with the massive treble hook. Pedrito winced at the pop the metal made as it punctured the fish's tough skin.

With the piece of fish on the hook, Don Pedro set it down again snatched one of his fishing poles from the bed of the truck. He attached a reel that had been sitting next to the tackle box and pulled the line through every loop. Once the line was ready, he tied the treble hook to it, using his teeth to tighten the knots. A smile bloomed under Don Pedro's thick, salt-and-pepper mustache as he held the hooked meat by the line toward his son.

"Mira, mijo, aquí tengo tu lunch," he said with a chuckle.

A large flap of skin dangled from the bait. Its dull brownish-olive color resembled a solid strip of water ripped from the Rio Grande, which Pedrito could see behind his father. The large, green vein reflected the sun in a way that made the boy think about a million shards of glass dancing with each other in perfect, impossible silence.

Pedrito's mind wandered. It always did when he was out by the river. He looked at his father and realized he looked just the way the books at the school's library told him Mexicans should look. The thought made him look down at the book he was holding in his lap. Pedrito loved books more than anything, and when his father told him they were going to go fishing for alligator gar as soon as school was out for the summer, he'd run to the library to ask them for a book about the subject. The lady had told him he had to wait for a week because they had to bring the book in from a different library, but it was worth the wait. The book contained pictures that made him daydream about reeling in a monster, a massive beast from the deepest, darkest hole in the river that would make him and his dad fishing legends. He imagined going to school with a copy of the newspaper, a photo of him and his dad with their colossal catch, beaming at the camera and looking like the heroes they were, right on the front page.

Don Pedro coughed. The sound yanked the boy back into his immediate reality. He looked at his father. He had finished baiting the second hook. He turned the lethal piece of fish this way and that in his brown hands, making sure the bait wasn't an easy meal for some brave, opportunistic fish. Finally, the man nodded. Pedrito knew that meant he was satisfied with the way the flesh concealed the sharp metal. Fishing, Don Pedro had told his son a few trips ago, is like life: mostly about deception, waiting, luck, and going home empty-handed. On this trip, he had also told his son that with fish as big as the alligator gar, they would have to use at least a 100-pound test line and that the hooks had to be as hard as they came.

"El pez caimán es una fantasma, Pedrito, vive en el agua muerta. Es difícil de agarrar porque no es de este mundo sino que se pasea entre éste y el más allá. It's better to think of it as a small monster y no un big fish. Así you're gonna be ready for anything, entiendes? El pez caimán es inteligente...very smart. That's why we have to hide the hook. Fishing is lying, and lying to a smart fish is almost impossible. We also have to see him before he sees us. He stays in the water, unmoving, like a log. Igualito que los caimanes. Sometimes you don't see it until it's too late. Most fish are stupid, but not this one. When you go fishing for pez caimán...you have to think of it as going to war with a man, not a fish."

Pedrito paid attention to every word his father said. The book on his lap, written by a man named David Joy, was packed with great pictures of massive alligator gars and stories about monstrous beasts pulled from the murky depths of rivers in Texas, Louisiana, Oklahoma, Arkansas, and Mississippi. Those stories, at least the parts he could understand, had fed the boy's imagination like gasoline thrown into a raging campfire. Unfortunately, the book also contained words like *ichthyological, fossilific,* and *stigma* that made it hard for him to understand. Whenever he couldn't make something out, he looked at the next picture or illustration and allowed his mind to fill in the blanks. His English was good, but not as good as it needed to be for him to fully comprehend everything that was written in those pages. As a result, the words that came from his father's mouth were crucial. For Pedrito, they were like a fishing course that would make him a great fisherman one day if he managed to pay attention and learn all the lessons. His father's voice was wrapped in reverence for the prehistoric fish and sprinkled with magic, mystery, and an inescapable sense of danger that gave the creature they were fishing for an almost mythical status, and the boy loved every minute of it.

Pedrito was quickly learning that there was nothing about the alligator gar in the book that his father couldn't tell him in simpler words, and nothing his father told him was new, because his grandfather had shared a thousand fishing stories from the creaking, perennially swaying comfort of his old rocking chair before going to sleep forever the previous summer. Both men knew the fish well. They had battled with it. They had felt the gliding, explosive strength of it straining against their landlocked muscles. They had seen its gigantic teeth perforate human skin. Pedrito knew they didn't really think the fish was a ghost that lived in dead water, but that telling him those things was the best way to teach him about the creature, the best way to get him to pay attention and prevent him from under-estimating the enormous fish and its mouthful of daggers.

"The best time of the year para agarrar un pez caimán is between Julio and August. That's when the water gets really hot and makes them a bit dumb, a bit confused. You know that feeling you get after eating too much pozole on a hot afternoon? Well, that's how they get on the hottest summer days. Ahí es cuando los podemos agarrar más fácil, mijo."

Pedrito heard the words and made a mental note, reminding himself that any comments about his father's accent or asking him to stick to Spanish would be like a slap in the face.

Don Pedro had once worked for a man who sold artisanal ponchos, sombreros, furniture, margarita glasses, and other handmade trinkets. Don Pedro knew a lot of artisans, so he became the middleman and learned a bit of English in the process. It made making money easier, and that was all the motivation he needed. He had even gone with Pedrito to the library in the city one day and gotten himself some cassettes that taught him the language. Three years ago he'd told his son he needed to start speaking English as much as possible so the gringos would think he had been born on their side of the border when they finally saved enough to pay the coyotes to take them across la frontera. According to his father, Pedrito had an aunt he'd never met who lived in El Paso and had a nice job, a big house, and a car that had three rows of seats. Pedrito was learning some English at school, and his father's pronunciation and constant Spanglish were atrocious, but he appreciated the effort. He was willing to do whatever it took to leave poverty and violence behind, and he knew that speaking English like a gabacho was crucial. He knew because his parents reminded him of it every single day.

"The hotter, the…more better it is for fishing for pez caimán, mijo. You want to find…aguas quietas, muertas, like this place here, places in the río where the water looks like it's not moving. Deep holes, yes? You look for places like this that have deep holes with calm water. Ahí es donde se esconden los fantasmas. They sit there and wait, como La Huesuda. You never know when they're going to strike, so you always have to be ready."

His father went on about how he needed to make sure to cast the bait straight into the middle of the deep hole and then let it hang without hitting the bottom. Getting it right could take a couple dozen tries. As with everything else in fishing, the trick was to not lose your patience.

"When we hear the chicharra go off, turn it off and let the fish take some line. The caimán, he wants to grab the bait and go away from the other fish, okay? Quiere correr. He's like a bad neighbor who wants to eat alone and doesn't like to share. Déjalo que se lleve 100 ó 200 yardas. When he stops, you make the line tight and then pull with everything you got. Como si quisieras sacar el pez del agua con un sólo jalón. That's how you set the hook in. If you pull before he stops running, you lose the fish. Si le enganchaste bien el anzuelo, ahí empieza la pelea. And try to be away from the water because that pelea is gonna be long and hard. I've seen many pescadores get tired and then get pulled into the water. Some come back out, but some don't. El río se los traga, y el río nunca devuelve las cosas intactas. You ready to do this?"

Pedrito nodded, a smile spreading across his face. It only took three casts before he landed the bait perfectly in the middle of the hole. Four more tries to get the depth right. He was proud of himself. He could read the same sentiment in his father's dark eyes, and it filled him with a joy for which he knew no words. After the last, perfect cast, they sat and waited. Don Pedro reached into the cooler, pulled out a can of beer, and cracked it open. Pedrito stared at the water, imagining a toothy monster smelling the fresh bait in that greenish darkness, waking up from a deep slumber, and slowly making its way to his baited hook.

Father and son quickly fell into that state of pregnant anticipation that all fishermen know so well. They both knew things could go from completely still to an explosion of adrenaline in a matter of seconds. While waiting for that to happen, Pedrito read a chapter from his book, his eyes taking breaks at the end of each paragraph to check for any movement in the water or tension on his line. Don Pedro drank, his eyes glued to the opposite side of the river, his mind trying hard not to think too much about the possibilities that waited for them there. Pedrito knew that time ceased to exist when they went fishing, and he liked it that way. They entered a strange stasis that prevented boredom, because action was always a bite away. When fishing, nothingness was full of possibility, quietness was a timeless inhalation before a scream, and inaction was just a fuse of indeterminate length before an explosion.

Fifteen minutes later, Don Pedro's line tensed. They both looked at the place where the line disappeared into the green water. The tiny ripples caused by the moving line meant something was happening on the other side of the green veil. Then the reel went off. There was a fish on the line.

The battle was much shorter than Pedrito expected. Like most animals, alligator gar start their lives as small versions of the giants they can eventually become, and they had hooked this one in its early stages. Don Pedro pulled the 3-foot gar onto land and bent over it carefully to remove the hook.

Then two things happened in the space contained by a single second: a loud crack startled Pedrito, and the top right half of Don Pedro's head vanished in a puff of red mist.

Don Pedro's body toppled sideways. Brain matter plopped out of the large hole in his skull. The man's black hair and the blood appearing around the wound's ragged edge accentuated the whiteness of his cranium. The fish flopped around a bit. Pedrito's scream rose until the air in his lungs ran out and his scream turned into silence. His body refused to move. His lungs ached. He inhaled. The earth's spinning pulled his feet one way as his head went the other.

Across the river, a tall white man wearing camouflage lowered his rifle. Pedrito saw movement, something unknown and large moving in his peripheral vision. He looked at the man and a second scream erupted from his throat. The man finished lowering the rifle and looked at Pedrito and then at Don Pedro's body. He cocked his head to the side like a dog trying to listen to something. He dropped the rifle. Pedrito's scream died and he inhaled warm, stale air that smelled like emptied bowels and blood seeping into the hot earth.

11

In a single, smooth motion, the tall man across the river reached behind him with his right hand, pulled a gun out of his pants, brought it to his right temple, and pulled the trigger. The sound was only half as bad as the one the rifle had made, but it had the same effect. The left side of the man's head exploded, sending a red and pink cloud into the air for a second before he crumbled to the ground.

Pedrito looked back at his father. His blood was now reaching the river, mixing on its way there with the blood coming from the gar's pierced mouth. The creature's teeth shone an impossibly sharp white under the Texas sun. Pedrito remained unmoving. Maybe he could disappear. Maybe if he respected the quietness of that moment, he would wake up to find his father fighting with a large gar. Then the fish flopped again and its movement shattered the fragile hope that had been building, impossible and forced, in the youngster's chest.

Pedrito's eyes darted to the fish. It was moving its mouth as if biting chunks out of the air. Then it left it opened wide, impossibly wide, and something dark, something like a breeze full of the echoes of shadows, exited its mouth. The dark mass of air floated up like a cloud of cigarette smoke that refused to vanish and then shot itself at Pedrito's face. Surprised by the sudden movement of a thing he didn't understand, the boy shook his head to the side and gasped. The third scream, which had been building inside him and was about to escape his throat and drown the world, never came. The sadness was still there, but Pedrito suddenly knew what he had to do to make it go away.

THE MOTHER

The Mother stared at the cracked ceiling and wished she could disappear into one of the fissures in the cement. She was focusing on trying to hear the sounds that usually came from outside her house. A cricket. A bird. The wind. A car. Someone's radio. A neighbor walking by. None of it came. The silence scared her. Finally, a dog barked twice somewhere in the distance, the sound tinged with hunger and desperation. The night swallowed the sound immediately, reminding the Mother where all complaints ultimately end up. With the barking extinguished, quietness returned, invading the space around her in a fraction of a second. It was an unnatural silence, the kind that loudly announces the presence of bad things or heralds the arrival of some catastrophe. It made the Mother nervous. Her hands refused to stay put, her fingers twitching, touching, moving over everything, even though she was looking for nothing.

When the sound of her own breathing became too much, the Mother decided to close her eyes and concentrate even harder on finding something else to keep the silence from becoming too oppressive. She breathed deeply, willed her heart to slow down. The house made a sound. It vanished. Then she picked up something else, something organic and somewhat rhythmic. The Boy's lungs. She'd found momentary salvation. She turned her head toward the sound and focused on the Boy's breathing, on the strange sense of security that came from having his thin body resting on the other side of the room.

The Boy inhaled.

Exhaled.

Inhaled.

The Boy snored for a second, air catching in the pinkness of his throat. The sound tilted upward as if accelerating, and then died down.

The polyrhythmic sound of air slowly entering and then leaving her son's body was the only other presence in the one-room abode, and it wasn't enough.

The Mother tried to remember the Boy's name, but it was still lost, swallowed by whatever was inside her, erased by the same force that had taken away the Father and then shown her his body. She didn't know what to call it, the thing that had forced her eyes closed and then filled her head with what she could only describe as a movie. It was a force. A spirit, maybe. An angry ghost. A cruel demon. Whatever it was, she knew it was evil, the kind of evil that turns machetes useless and laughs at guns.

Guilt ate at her with sharp, relentless teeth. She had given life to the Boy, but now the thing she was turning into had taken his name from her. She wondered what the Father would say about that. His name had been the first to go, but the images that had popped into her brain when he died were unforgettable.

She moved around on the bed, readjusting limbs that never felt comfortable. Her arms were alien appendages she didn't know what to do with. She opened her eyes briefly just to make sure the darkness around her was still familiar, and then closed them again and remembered the Father. She saw the bloated face, the tied hands resembling puppet limbs, the lifeless body falling into a hole in the ground, quickly finding its place on top of the bodies already there. She knew it was true despite not knowing why she had been able to see it all so clearly. Seeing the face of the Father had broken her, but that was nothing compared to the other people she saw, to the knowledge that the Father was just another grain of sand in an expanding beach of unspeakable atrocity. What had really pushed the Mother to the edge of insanity had been the bodies already in the grave. The number of dead people in the hole was alarming, but the worst of it was the force of all those lives turned into a pile of rotting flesh stuffed in a hole in the desert.

The Mother knew that clandestine communal graves were like black holes that folks got sucked into and disappeared forever, and her husband had been thrown into one. He had been swallowed by the darkness, turned into a statistic, absorbed by the earth, vanished forever into a collective mass of decay and silence. Her husband had become empty space, a missing body, a mere memory. His love, or the somewhat domesticated civility they had come to share, had been ripped out of her. Now the thing invading her body, the last remains of the Father's actions on this earth, had fed on the pain and anguish that had invaded that empty space in her chest.

For the past few nights, the Mother had contemplated emptiness. She felt hollow despite her round, taut belly and the stirring creature inside it. During her first pregnancy, she'd felt like a magical vessel, a caregiver tasked with bringing life into the world. Even when the vomiting came and the smell of uncooked chicken made her gag, she had felt that her state was a good thing. Even through the pain and the blood and the screaming, bringing a life into the world had made her feel powerful and full of magic; una bruja de la tierra regalándole un milagro al universe. This time, it felt different. It felt wrong. The thing inside her felt more like a trespasser, an unwelcome guest, a parasite. With no husband and a slithering intruder in her guts that she couldn't bring herself to think of as her baby, all that was left was emptiness, an all-consuming hollowness that she couldn't fill regardless of what she did or thought. She moved, worked, and took care of her son, but all that movement was just an illusion. Her actions were of no consequence. She was stuck in a perennial state of agitated stagnation. Now her body was falling into a similar state.

She remembered a movie she'd seen years ago with her husband. In it, people in a spaceship encountered a different, long-lost vessel that had been lost in the endless blackness for many years. It was full of death, and contaminated with something so evil that time and space meant nothing to it. She felt like that lost craft: infected by something evil beyond time. The feeling, and the memories of that horrendous film, were the last things she needed, so the

Mother shook the thoughts away and opened her eyes to look around at the darkness, the walls, and her son.

Like every preceding night, the Mother had spent the afternoon trapped between conflicting feelings. She was glad to see the sun disappear over the horizon, because the darkness that fell on the outskirts of Nuevo Laredo combined with the heat of summer to cover everything in something akin to a wet towel that signaled the end of the day, and she was glad for the momentary respite, despite knowing that there was still something coming, something that made the wish for escape into oblivion dance at the periphery of her thoughts. However, she was also afraid of everything that would fill the hours before the sun came back to bathe the small house with its yellow warmth. Her eyes darted around in the dark, looking for a way out of something she didn't fully comprehend.

On the other side of the room, the Boy scratched his head, moved his hands around, bunched his pillow under his face, moaned, and snorted snot back into his skull. The Mother wondered about the continuing efficacy of the small things that stood between her immediate reality and any action aimed at satisfying her thirst for long-term un-consciousness. A few days before, the idea of killing her son and then taking her own life had briefly crossed her mind.

It felt sudden and inevitable, like looking up at the sky and seeing a bird mid-flight. Since then, she had been lying to herself, pretending that the memory of that thought didn't exist, feigning that survival is morally superior to a voluntary exit from this plane of existence.

The Boy stopped moving, settled, and once again became a lumpy shadow. His breathing regained its slow rhythm, a sound that invited her to relax. She couldn't. A nightmare was rolling around in her womb. She lied to herself again, repeated like a mantra that it was nothing more than dinner, an upset stomach, a weird pregnancy glitch. The Mother and the Boy had eaten a plate of beans with ham and made small talk about plans for the following day. Their words were vacuous, but there was something comforting in their familiar cadence. At last, they had both washed their faces and mouths, changed into more comfortable attire, and laid down in their respective beds. That's when the fear started creeping into her system.

For a few minutes, the Mother entertained herself by trying to remember every detail of the day. Then she focused on the Boy's movements and, when those started to become few and far between, she turned her attention to the aches invading her body. She imagined them as wounds that could be quickly healed by the power of work. Then she accepted the painful truth: work was what caused her the aches in the first place. As the tension of the day slowly evaporated like the morning fog when the sun caresses the river, her body became everything. But focusing on her body was a mistake. The thing inside her began to stir. The Mother closed her eyes and prayed to a God she believed in less with each passing day.

"No me hagas esto, Padrecito. Por favor, te lo suplico."

She had been sleeping the first time the thing inside her had slithered out and later reentered her body. Her brain had screamed at her to wake up, told her she was losing the baby. Instinctively, she had reached down. Her hands found something hard, slimy, and round protruding from the space between her legs. Then she had felt sharp teeth clamp down on the side of her hand, perforating the tough, overworked skin. She had gasped, pulled her hand away. A shiver had run down her spine like cold water and fear had constricted her scalp, making her feel like her skull was two sizes too big for her head. The horror in her veins had frozen her, leaving her immobile, even beyond shivering. With a sound like a shoe caught in the mud, the creature finally exited her body. She had stayed there, breathing heavily, trying to decide if what had happened was real or the most vivid nightmare she'd ever had. She had closed her

21

eyes, a half-forgotten prayer for protection caught around her teeth, and placed her trembling hands atop her vacated stomach. The emptiness she felt there, right beneath her loose skin and yet a million miles away, was all the answer she'd needed.

In bed, surrounded by darkness and silence, the memory of that first time floating above her *felt* like a threat, but it soon became a physical reality. The Mother felt the thing begin to stir. The feeling reminded her of indigestion, but the grumbling and bubbling happened beneath her stomach. Then, the thing started to slide out. Its width was enough to be uncomfortable, but not too painful. This time, she decided to try to at least catch a glimpse of it. More than curiosity, she wanted visual proof that her sanity, while damaged, still existed.

Ten seconds later, the creature was out. The Mother propped herself up on her right elbow and looked around the room. She saw it near the door: a long, grey, slimy body. She immediately thought of an eel. An overfed, veiny eel with a large mouth and no eyes. The scant light coming through the window above the Boy's bed reflected off the thing's skin. It sat there, suspended in time like a monster remembered from a childhood movie. Then it began to shake violently, its wet body slapping against the floor like a fish pulled from the water. Small legs with what looked like baby hands sprouted from four spots in the creature's body. In a moment, it stopped resembling an eel and morphed into a shape reminiscent of a salamander. The Mother closed her eyes. There was a scream somewhere in her chest, but fear and surprise were pushing it back, drowning it as violently as La Llorona drowned her babies. Her brain started naming saints, asking for help, praying for forgiveness for whatever awful sin she had committed. When she looked back, the thing was gone.

She had no idea how or why the thing had sprouted limbs. The somewhat reptilian baby hands had freaked her out more than the mouth full of small, sharp teeth, but she instinctively knew she had reached a space beyond simple explanations, a place that rendered questions useless, mere frustrating exercises in futility. She had paid attention every night, and she was sure there had been no limbs on it when it exited or reentered her, so what her eyes had seen had to be true.

The Boy moaned again, as if the sacred bond between mother and son somehow communicated to him the anguish she was feeling. She took a deep breath and settled in to wait for the parasite's return. She knew she had to put a stop to it, and feared that not doing it in time would lead to her giving birth to something not of this world, something that would bring death and destruction to Nuevo Laredo and beyond.

THE COYOTE

The truck stopped in the middle of the desert with a metallic groan. It rattled as if it wasn't ready to stop after so many miles. The man inside waited a moment before opening the door. The damn dust would get on everything and cover his boots with a thick brown layer that he'd have to hose down, but there was no reason to make it worse. After a minute, the dust settled a bit, just like the truck had. "La inercia es el milagro nuestro de cada día," the man whispered to himself.

The other opened slowly, the rust in the door's hinges making the metal sing a painful song. The man climbed down, adjusted his pants, and made his way to the back of the truck.

The coyote opened the doors. The harsh light blinded the four kids cowering in the back. They squinted and raised their hands to their faces like vampires about to start bubbling under the Texas sun.

"Abajo," said the man, looking at the four Salvadorans, wondering how in the world the two younger ones survived a ride in La Bestia. Images of his own harrowing trip came to him, sending a shot of anger and adrenaline into his veins with stampeding force. He spat on the dirt and pondered which of the kids had been raped. He searched their scrunched faces for that look of resignation, that invisible-yet-visible shadow that forever twisted the faces of those who survive the worst kind of abuse imaginable. He felt awful for trying to figure it out, but he knew the anger would push him forward and help him keep on doing the Lord's work. He also knew that, in a group of four, at least one had probably suffered at the hands of some demon in human form. Facts are harder to swallow than rocks, but just as solid. Standing there, looking at those scared kids, he thought about taking a ride in La Bestia and collecting testicles in the name of decency, but he knew he didn't have the time. Plus, decency didn't put money in anyone's pockets, and castrating rapists doesn't help get children across the border.

The coyote stepped away from the door and watched as the kids made their way to the edge and carefully jumped down, their legs weak from the trip, lack of food, and fear. The coyote helped the youngest one, the only girl, jump down to the ground. She thanked him in a cracked voice that reminded him of those dolls that talk after you pull a string on their back.

"You and you, come with me," the man barked while pointing at the two oldest boys. The anger in his voice coming from the fact that he already hated what would come next.

The two oldest kids looked at each other and started walking behind the coyote, following him toward the front of the truck. One was about fourteen. Short for his age. He had yellow teeth and the kind of acne that turns youth into an endless nightmare and fills souls with hatred. The other was seventeen or so. Tall. All bones and a few lines that promised future muscles once he started eating well. This was the one the coyote worried about. He had already explained to them what would happen, but you never know what people will do after you put your hands on them. Underestimating people was something he'd seen too many idiots do, and he never made that mistake.

They reached the front of the truck and the man stopped. He kept his back to the kids. He wanted to give them a good look at the Guadalupana emblazoned on the back of his shirt. La Virgencita would bless them, he was sure of it. He could feel the kids looking at his back, taking in La Virgencita with her two guns. Finally, he turned around. The teens stood side by side, looking like they were ready to hold hands and start crying. The coyote dug into the right pocket of his jeans and pulled out his brass knuckles. They were round at the top, shiny under the midday sun. The kids took a step back simultaneously when he slid them on.

"Tranquilos. I'll only hurt you a bit. You know how it is, esto lo hago por su propio bien," he said. The coyote brought his hand up and the brass knuckles caught the sun again, stabbed him in the eyes. He convinced himself that was a sign from God to carry on, to use the strange tool on the kids in the name of salvation. He nodded, crossed himself, said, "Gracias, Padrecito, en tu nombre sagrado encomiendo mi trabajo" under his breath. *God works in mysterious ways,* thought the coyote for a second, *but he gets really fucking weird when it comes to poor people and dangerous places.*

The coyote had been doing the same thing for years. By now he had mastered the art of hurting kids just enough to get the job done. Hit them too hard and you run risks. On his second trip, a child lost an eye. That was too much. Hit them too soft and they'll be fully healed by the time they finally get to go through the interview at the icebox.

If they look too good, too healthy, the fucking gringos will do everything in their power to send them back to whatever hell they came from. Hurt them just right and a better future will make their scars feel like blessings. Pain is sometimes the only path to deliverance.

"Okay, remember: you were victims of gang violence. Los Malditos, la Salvatrucha, Calle 18…I don't care. You pick one and stick to it. Repitan el mismo cuento siempre. Explain to them: they attack you regularly. Tienen miedo de que los maten. Digan que mataron a un hermano suyo o algo. Violaron a su madrecita. Raptaron a su hermana. Lo que sea. And make sure you show them your wounds, got it?"

The kids nodded. The coyote looked down and then shot a straight right at the older kid. He felt his nose crunch under the brass knuckles. The kid took two steps back and dropped, his hands cradling his face, a sound that belonged in the throat of a calf erupting from his covered mouth. The coyote knew that surprising them was the only way to go. He looked at the younger kid. A piss stain was spreading down the front of his pants. The man grabbed him by the hair and pulled as he brought his right knee up, sinking it into the kid's stomach. The tiny body crumbled like someone had pulled its plug. He wouldn't run away after that. The coyote bent down, aimed for the right ear, and popped him twice. Hard. The ear split, started bleeding. A round bump immediately began to change the shape of the youngster's head. That would last him a few days. It was a good one. It would turn purple, then blue, and finally green before acquiring a ghostly yellowish hue and disappearing from his body, if not from his memory. The hit would definitely still be there when he went through the interview. Maybe not the whole thing, but at least one of those shades would still be coloring his skin when la pinche migra took a look at him. The coyote stopped thinking about the future and used his left hand to bust the kid's lower lip open. He had to take care not to fuck his teeth up too much, so he used that hand instead of the one accentuated by metal. He felt teeth bite into his knuckles, almost piercing the skin. He punched again, just to make sure the lip split enough to leave a lasting wound.

The older kid was still down, holding his face, moaning. Blood ran down his chin and neck. A thick mixture of blood, tears, and snot stained his shirt. Good thing the man had clean clothes for them, or the whole thing would be too obvious. The coyote knew that, because he was at the edge of adulthood, this one would have a harder time with la migra. The amount of pity you generate in others diminishes with every birthday. People, the coyote knew,

29

are like food: the closer you get to your expiration date, the less others are drawn to you. This kid was too close to adulthood to be seen as a kid, and thus would be treated like an adult. He needed to be hurt bad in order to really sell the sad story, to pull eyes away from the fading remnants of his boyhood and the incipient facial hair and onto the scabs on his face, the pain, brutality, and promises of death quietly resting inside his healing wounds. At least his English was better than the rest of them; that would help him sell his story.

The coyote walked up to the writhing teenager, turned him sideways with his boot, and landed three hard kicks to his upper back. The pointy boots would break the skin or at least leave a good bruise. No one would think of those wounds as something he did to himself. Then he kneeled, slapped the teenager's hands away, and punched him in the face three times. The first punch got another crack out of the nose and left it slightly bent to the left. The kid instinctively brought his hands up again. There was a loud snap after the second punch that told the coyote the hit had broken a finger. He aimed higher for the third and went sideways with a mean hook. The brass knuckles landed where the kid's eyebrow ended. The flesh there cracked open like a bizarre smile and blood started pouring out. That would do.

Once both kids got up, the coyote brought them a gallon of water and a dirty towel to clean themselves. He also handed them some unsoiled clothes. He used a corner of the towel to clean the blood off his brass knuckles and hands. Then he pulled out the small vial of styptic powder he always carried around on jobs and applied some to the kid's busted eyebrow, which kept bleeding profusely.

Once they looked almost normal again, he addressed them. "Now you walk. Hasta que se topen con la migra. Once you see the Border Patrol, go to them. If you don't wanna go back, remember: los mareros are looking for you. You fear for your life and get beat regularly. No tienen nada ni nadie a quién regresar, entendido?"

A few grunts and nods was all he got from them. That was fine. He didn't expect more. The wounds were still too fresh, and fear gnawed at them like a hungry dog.

The coyote looked at them again and sent a silent prayer up to the blue, endless sky. Not much else he could do now except give them some drinking water for the trip ahead and point them in the right direction. "En tus manos los dejo, Padre," he whispered to himself, feeling La Virgencita on his back radiating strength into his body.

At the back of the truck, the little girl looked at him with fire in her eyes. She had heard everything. The coy-

31

ote hoped that fire would be enough to keep her safe. He kneeled in front of her.

"I'm one of the good guys, mija. Probablemente lo más cercano a un ángel que vas a conocer en tu vida. Listen, anyone touches you, you put your nails in his eyes and kick him right here," he said, patting his crotch. "And stay close to these guys. Que la Virgencita te lleve de la mano por el camino que tienes por delante."

The four kids stared walking away. The coyote knew they would look back at him and be surprised they didn't get killed like so many others. No, they belonged to the lucky few who made it. Watching them take their first steps in the promised land was always great, but the coyote wouldn't stick around to watch them walk away. There were more kids waiting for him. He needed to get moving. He was doing God's work, and the Devil tended to move quickly when you weren't looking.

JAIME

The smell of freedom. People talked about it like it was real. Jaime wished it was. He only smelled the rotten stink of mold and the ammonia odor of cat piss that had taken over the small room where most of his stuff was packed in cardboard boxes marked "Charmin toilet tissue."

Nothing was happening and that felt like too much. Everything was nothing and too much all at once and that brought with it a sense of frustration sprinkled with depression that he hadn't felt since his first couple days in a cell. He was too aware of everything, and everything bothered him. The stench. The oppressive summer heat. The wobbly clatter of a ceiling fan that uselessly sliced warm air. The dust bunnies screaming. His mom hadn't cleaned his room before picking him up. Through the window, a light breeze brought from the garage the smell of gasoline and

33

neglected things that should have been thrown away a long time ago. It all fueled Jaime's anger. He was angry that he got caught and locked away for four years. He was angry that while inside his tough guy persona had crumbled and only a friend's cousin had kept his ass from being used as an entertainment center by larger, older, meaner inmates. He was angry that his mom stayed with her abusive boyfriend through the whole fucking ordeal and had only visited him once, claiming the three-hour drive was too much and she couldn't see him like that because it broke her heart. He was angry because that same boyfriend, Cookie, had made the damn call that had gotten him locked up, just so he could get him out of the way for a while. He was angry that he never cared enough to ask how a sack of blubber ended up with that ridiculous nickname. Galletita.

Pinche pendejo. But most of all, Jaime was angry about his current state. He had plans while inside, but couldn't remember any of them. He wanted to go places where he hadn't fucked up yet and accomplish something. He wanted to travel and work and experience new things. He wanted to live his freedom the way others live theirs, like life is a fucking celebration, like being alive is worth it, like every new day is a new gift full of opportunities and good things. But he couldn't do any of that now that there were no locks on the doors, no guards, no walls, no towers topped with angry snipers that would've loved to put a bullet in his brain. No, the only thing he could do was wonder why he couldn't do anything now, why he felt like he was frozen, and why that frozen feeling locked him in place and forced him to stay in his room, without the need for barbed-wire fences or guards.

The second day after Jamie's release from prison, his cousin Eduardo called from San Antonio. Eduardo said he was making bank running meth for La Eme. All Jaime had to do is get to San Antonio and there would be a job waiting for him. An easy job. Good money. Women. Connections. However, to his surprise, he sat down after the call and realized he didn't want to go. He wanted out. He wanted peace of mind. That's all he wanted, and nothing seemed attainable. He thought being out would do the trick, but it didn't. In fact, the first thing he did after getting home was go through his things and get his piece. He cleaned, oiled, and loaded it. You can leave the big house, but you carry some of the fear for the rest of your life, like a prison tattoo on your soul. He ran his hands down his face. He looked at the damn useless fan. He was stuck, sweaty, and angry, looking at his gun and trying to ignore how easy it'd be to use it to get enough money for his own place, someplace far away from all the memories and his mother's constant coughing and the rotten smell of the carpet and fucking Cookie. He sat up and shook his head like a madman. That stopped his crazy thoughts for a few blessed seconds.

Leaving the room was a bad idea, but staying cooped up in there was worse. Jaime told himself to move.

Muévete, pendejo.

Haz algo.

Take a leak.

Drink some water.

Wash your face.

Make a phone call that matters.

Check the fridge.

He knew those simple tasks would help him escape the trap he was setting himself. Unfortunately, moving his body struck him as an impossibility, something that could only be accomplished with the help of a few strong men. Finally, Jaime got out of bed, opened the door, and walked out of his room.

The living room was at the end of the short hallway. His mom and Cookie had been in there most of the day, watching television and smoking cigarettes like they were going out of style. The smoke was so thick Jaime wondered if he'd have to pull it apart with his hands to get to the kitchen.

"Ahí vas, a buscar un poco más de comida gratis, como el sinvergüenza que eres," said Cookie. "Hace dos días y medio que llegastes y no has hecho ni una pinche llamada para ver si alguien te puede conseguir un jale."

Jaime ignored him. He didn't need to hear this crap from the man who probably sent him away. It was too much to deal with. Plus, his mother's silence, the one from when they took him away in handcuffs and the one resting like a fat cat inside her mouth while Cookie talked shit at him, felt like a burn, like acid coating the skin of his chest and face.

The kitchen smelled worse than the rest of the house. Next to the fridge stood three litter boxes full of solidified feces. Jaime grabbed a glass from the cupboard and filled it with tap water.

"Oye, pendejo, te estaba hablando," said Cookie.

Jaime turned around. The fat man stood behind him, his breath a mix of cheap beer, cigarettes, raw onions, and gingivitis that somehow overpowered the combined stench of cat piss and skipped showers. Jaime took a step back, hoping for fresh air. Cookie laughed, a golden crown shining a bit inside a mouth full of brown and yellow teeth. In that laugh, Jaime saw things. Bad things. This motherfucker made the call. It had to have been him. None of Jamie's homies would have ratted him out like that, and his mom, despite her silences, would die before hurting him, so the fat, smelly bastard had to be the one. Cookie's laughter turned into a hacking cough. His disgustingly huge panza bounced inside the stretched brown fabric of his T-shirt.

"Buscaré trabajo el lunes," said Jaime. "Tengo un cuate de la prepa que…"

"Ninguno de tus pinches amigos te puede conseguir una buena chamba y lo sabes."

"Si Jaime dice que va a buscar trabajo, va a buscar trabajo," said Lorena, Jaime's mother, from somewhere behind the fat man. Then she stood there, five foot nothing, burying her eyes into Cookie. A cigarette dangled from her lips. There were more lines around her eyes than Jaime remembered, but the bun on top of her head was still as dark as midnight during a blackout on a night with no moon.

Both men were surprised to hear her. Cookie turned around and hissed something a couple of inches from Lorena's face. She walked away. Cookie followed her into the living room. Jaime saw an opportunity to disappear before his anger took over. He left the kitchen and crossed the living room while staring at the filthy carpet. He reached his door.

Slap.

The sound stopped him in his tracks. Was that the TV? He looked back down the hallway. His mother was making her way to the bathroom. She looked pissed. He knew the fresh red blemishes on her cheek and neck weren't from being in the kitchen or out in the Texas heat. Neither were the few hairs that had popped out of her bun like tiny black antennas. Something in his chest tensed like a guitar string and his lungs felt too small. Cookie stepped out of their room, grabbed Lorena's arm, and yanked her back. She stumbled.

"No voy a permitir que trates a ese puto criminal como a un bebé," said Cookie.

Instead of replying, Lorena took another step toward the bathroom. Cookie grabbed her again, pulled her close, and didn't let go this time. Jaime watched as the fat man placed his mouth close to his mother's ear and whispered something. She replied with the same hushed tone, something about it being her house, not his. Whatever it was, her words had consequences. Cookie looked hurt, moved his head back like someone smelling something rotten. He pushed her away and followed it up with another slap. Jaime was in front of Cookie before realizing he had moved. The fat man smiled at him. Jaime took in his bald head, the beads of oily beer sweat dotting his forehead, his cracked lips, and the incongruent shiny tooth in his dental cemetery.

Jamie's jaw clenched but he managed to spit out some words. "Si la vuelves a tocar…"

Cookie's grin grew wider. "No te atrevas a amenazarme, culero. Esta puede ser la casa de tu madre, pero el que paga las cuentas aquí soy yo, así que hago lo que me da la gana."

Jaime had been tempted to punch his mother's boyfriend many times, but knew he'd end up being the one getting kicked out of the house if he ever did. Somewhere between realizing Cookie had been the one who called the cops and the second slap the asshole gave his mother, however, that concern had vanished. He didn't care. He'd been buried and crawled back from the hole, a survivor. He had no home and made the shadows his refuge. The man who sent him away stood in front of him, and that made everything else disappear. Cookie was responsible for the anger, the lost time, the fear. He was responsible for the red welts on his mother's face and neck. He was responsible for a criminal record that would make getting a job much harder.

The first punch was a right hook, fast and tight, the way he learned to punch in prison. His fist closed Cookie's mouth shut with a crack and snapped his head back. The fat man stumbled, but didn't go down. He looked forward. Surprise, fear, and rage battled on his face and eyes, jockeying for control of his features. He started to bring his hands up, his movements slowed by surprise and years of piled fat.

The second punch was a straight right that slipped between the Cookie's hands. Cartilage crunched. Blood gushed. His legs gave out and he flopped onto his back.

Jaime kneeled, grabbed Cookie's head by the ears, and slammed it against the carpet. The thud was too dull, too kind, so he threw a leg over his chest, sat on the man, and started punching.

Jaime was aware of his mother screaming. He felt her nails digging into his arms and shoulders from the back, but none of it mattered. He was finally moving, doing something. No more stagnation. Then Lorena left him alone, took her screaming elsewhere. Jaime kept punching until Cookie's nose was no more. The man emitted a guttural moan that sounded like a small mammal drowning in pancake syrup. A jagged piece of bone poked out from the pulpy red mess that used to be Cookie's right eye. It stabbed Jaime's hand and he pulled back. His hands trembled. His knuckles bled. His lungs ached. His right fist hurt more than anything he could remember. He had to keep moving, so he stood up and went to the bathroom.

The water from the bathroom's faucet was colder than the kitchen's. Jaime could hear his mother sobbing, talking, hiccupping. Jaime washed his hands and splashed water on his face. The cuts on his knuckles went white, then pink, and finally started bleeding again. He would take care of that later.

A siren wailed somewhere in the distance and weaved into Lorena's lamentations. Jaime sat on the toilet and tried to recall the things he had wanted to do when he finally got out, but nothing came. Behind his mother, on the small table with the vase that never held any flowers, were some keys. Cookie's car keys. Jaime left the bathroom, hustled past his crying mother, and grabbed the keys. The car sat at the curb, like always, because the garage was full of clutter. It was an ugly, dirty, purple 2004 Impala SS. He briefly recalled Cookie complaining about the purple paint job he had done to it. The bastard loved that car more than he ever loved his mother. Jaime looked at its pretentious chrome rims and hoped there was plenty of gas in the tank because he was going wherever he had to go to stay out of prison.

He was about to take a step toward the car when he remembered the gun on top of his bed. He sprinted into his room, grabbed the piece, and ran out to the car.

ALMA

The stack of bills reminded Alma of a lopsided tower of pancakes. Her stomach grumbled. She ignored the sound and stared back at her laptop's screen. A thin black line pulsated at the top of a blank Word document. Alma had an idea for a performance piece, something that would make people sit up and take notice, but the right words refused to come. The idea was there, an unformed thing waiting for her to shape it into words, but the space it had to travel to get from her brain to the page was apparently plagued by hungry predators. The process, as always, was frustrating her beyond words. If she couldn't convince institutions to give her money, or at least a free space to perform the piece, her idea would stay an idea, instead of becoming art. And her career would remain a promise, something that could be, stuck between the world of dreams and everyday reality.

Every time she sat down to write and the words refused to flow, Alma thought about making another YouTube video. Years ago she had made her first one. She had been angry at the lack of strong concepts in contemporary performance art, and her answer to that, a critique of sorts that flew like an angry bird way above most heads, had been to dress like a chola, get in front of her phone's camera, and chug an entire large bottle of Cholula. She wanted to show the world the embodiment of their collective, media-created, imaginary version of most Mexican women consuming a product they identified as Mexican but that had the cultural legitimacy of Taco Bell. Within hours of uploading it to YouTube, the video had gone viral. It was funny. Some thought it was strong. No one cared that it was a critique. No one cared that she was a black Puerto Rican and not Mexican. No one cared that she had a hundred ideas that were better than that. A few days later, everyone had forgotten about it. Since then, she'd done a few more videos, but now she wanted to do something much larger, something that would get her interviews and put money in her pocket.

Alma knew that blood and sex were the way to sell. The title for her next piece had been the first thing to come to her: "Fucking/Gringos/Fucking/Me." She wanted to critique white culture under Trump, to eviscerate bland arguments that tried to veil latent xenophobia. She wanted to shine a light on the institutionalized racism that made this country a pain for anyone on the "wrong" side of Otherness. She wanted to insult the men who constantly turned her black skin into a fetish and joked about how fiery Latinas were supposed to be. She wanted to destroy the border wall before the first move was made to actually build anything resembling it, by showing that women are one across the world. She wanted to show her white liberal friends how some of their discourses were thinly-cloaked attempts to make up for their racist families or white guilt or just crap they'd picked up from popular television personalities and later regurgitated with ludicrous levels of self-assuredness and conviction. Most of all, she wanted to do all that in the context of her body, a body that suffered figurative and literal attempts to fuck her/it every single day, a body that was culturally forced to dance between the desire expressed for it by some and the desire to expel it expressed by others. Her body, her Black, multicultural, bilingual, Caribbean body was at once a shrine and a weapon, and she wanted to show and celebrate that duality.

The piece would end with some special effects. She'd already learned she could tape bags of fake blood to her skin to make it look real. The grand finale would be an explosion of blood. They wanted to fuck her? Well, she was going to fuck herself in their name. She was going to defile her body, to put an end to the invasion they blamed her for despite her blue passport, and she would do it all with a machete. That would make a powerful statement. If she made it violent enough, folks would talk about it. All she needed was a good month in a free venue and she'd make enough to carry her for the next six months as she worked on smaller projects and allowed her big ideas to coalesce into the next big performance. Unfortunately, before any of that happened, she had to write a convincing artist's manifesto and a clear, powerful synopsis that would later have to land in the right inbox, along with all the other bullshit they ask for in every single grant.

Alma looked back at the stack of bills next to the mouse pad. Electricity. Internet. Water. Phone. Rent. Gas. Student loans. Car insurance. It was all too much. Anger flared in her chest. She looked back at the screen and wrote.

"Sometimes the drums beating in my blood get too loud. They take over and silence all the other nonsense, all the other things trying to distract me with their immediacy, their apparent ties to the apocalypse, their loud, obnoxious wrongness. When that happens, I close my eyes and listen to my blood, and when I do that, this is what I hear:

I hear the drums, the stretched skins of dead animals, thrumming powerfully, undeniably through my veins, carrying with them the songs of lost people, mixed cultures, and a plethora of angry gods hidden inside the new deities the Spaniards imposed on two thirds of my DNA.

I hear the strength of my great-great-great-grandmother, who escaped slavery across a deadly river that poetess Julia de Burgos later loved with her cuerpo y alma. I hear her voice in my blood say that no person should ever be owned and that laughing in the face of death is better than having to live as abused property.

I hear the labor and the love and the blood and the patience of generations of women who fought for better days and more opportunities and less hunger and more justice. I hear the soft rasping sound made by the calloused hands of men who battled to put food on the table and did all they could to make sure their kids grew up knowing the difference between right and wrong. I hear them all saying I need to remember everything, especially because I am the migrant daughter of a migrant, the daughter of a mother whose DNA carries the knowledge of escape and the fear and hatred that comes from abused flesh, from the whistling of the whip in the air.

I hear the world spinning as poems are written and babies are born and bullets fly and music is made and jobs are lost and spells are cast and cars crash and alcohol disappears down gullets and leaves fall to the ground and alley cats sing to the night with voices they borrow from depressed demons and hatred tries to win the battle and inspiration vanishes and a kid becomes a walking miracle as she crosses the border without being raped or abused or denigrated and an angry lover puts his vengeance inside a sharp blade and water flows full of memories from its eternal recycling and some nameless bird bathes in it before a homeless man drops a cigarette butt that will end up in the creek, mixed in with all that eternal return.

I hear the obscene screams of angry gods who were forced to dress their black skin in whiteness to survive once their devotees were brought to the Caribbean. Their strength is there, coursing through the streets like the blood courses through my veins, because we still call their names, pray to them, light candles, offer them tiny deaths and food and fire and dreams.

I hear a special kind of magic that has to do with the earth, with everyday occurrences, with wisdom and pain. I hear the silence of decapitated chickens and photos left in water overnight and the black insides of an egg after a limpia and the shivering leaves of rompe saragüey and ya tú sabes que con los santos no se juega.

I hear a whole house shaking and groaning as a train to who knows where rattles by on the too-close tracks as my grandmother pets an unnamed cat and adjusts her glasses on her almost useless eyes with hands covered in a mixture of lines and scars that heal you with their touch. I hear her spirit hovering above me, raining love down on my head, reminding me that wounds become scars that become stories that become herstory. Reminding me that nothing is free. Reminding me that my skin is a miracle and my soul its own deity and my future a malleable thing I can shape with sweat and blood and tears and effort.

I hear my other grandmother saying that the bathroom in the hallway belongs to the spirits, a los muertos, and the saints. Never blow out those candles, she says. *Never forget your prayers, mijita,* she reminds me. *Never put your own purse or let the other women in your life put their purses on the ground. Never take a pregnant woman to a funeral, mija. Never leave your milagritos at home,* she repeats, pulling her dress to the side to reveal a hundred tiny pieces of metal pulling at her bra. I hear her laugh and I hear her telling me to let dogs lick my wounds because that worked for San Lázaro and thus it will work for me. She tells me this as the huge statue of San Lázaro looks on, black, tall, emaciated, and surrounded by a pack of skinny dogs I'll never forget. He is my fear and redemption. He embodies syncretism and childhood and faith. He is the Holy Poor. He is the Holy Black.

I hear the aching eloquence of my father's silence as he drinks in the kitchen, cloaked in darkness, a million miles from home, probably regretting passing on to me the invisible gene that makes us nomads, hardheaded hustlers, beautiful, flawed creatures that are too quick to love and too quick to anger.

I hear my mother crying after calling the cops on me for fighting a girl in our barrio and threatening her with a knife and then laughing after lying to the cops for me and crying because my sister is doing things that never lead to good things and so am I and, carajo, she tried with all she had but sometimes all you have is not nearly enough.

I hear an endless succession of planes taking off and landing and more or less creating the fabric of life with their constant motion, their incessant pregnancy with all of us, their hunger for goodbyes and tears and promises.

I hear an old lady saying "Que Dios te bendiga, mija" while another says "Tranquila, niña, que Elegguá abre el camino." And then comes the holy music. Rubén Blades.

Héctor Lavoe. Roberto Roena. Celia Cruz. Frankie Ruíz. Eddie Palmieri. Y después el gran Maelo, reminding me I'm still alive:

> *De las tumbas quiero irme*
> *No sé cuando pasará*
> *Las tumbas son pa' los muertos*
> *Y de muerto no tengo na.*

I hear salsa and flamenco, reggae and merengue, rock and bachata, nueva trova and jazz.

I hear the streets of Rio Piedras dancing to their own hot rhythm, the cobblestones of Viejo San Juan cracking under the weight of history and oppression, the cries of a pueblo that grew up as a colony and stayed there like a useless daughter who lacks the strength to move out, to learn that some things are better left in the past. I hear Yukiyú screaming and floods and crying and parties and dominoes clacking together and violence and beauty and hurricanes and that thing in my chest that calls me home every day.

I hear waves and sweat and drunk afternoons and meat sizzling on a grill and someone vomiting out their pain and someone praying as they yank the head off a chicken and my grandma asking for blessings for the dead as we drive past a cemetery and a chord on a guitar with one finger in the wrong place and brakes screaming in the distance and the laughter of my friends at home, their skins and hair and eyes of every color imaginable and then the song of the coquí signaling another trip around the sun and finally guns going off in the Luis Lloréns Torres projects as I drift off to sleep. I hear someone explain that the things you love can haunt you, and vice versa.

I hear a young woman who looks like me rezando un Padre Nuestro as an old black man dressed in white sends his own prayers to the sky: Obatalá obá layé ela iwo alara ache.

I hear "Where are you originally from?" and "Where is your accent from?" and "Wow, you're so eloquent!" and "You're very pretty…for a dark girl" and "Are you Mexican?" and "Are you from Jamaica?" and "Is one of your parents white?" and "Nice hair! Can I touch it?" and a million other dumb comments that scholars say I should call *microaggressions* but that sometimes feel anything but micro.

I hear my own anger claiming that I am a daughter of Changó while the sound of a bagpipe reaches into my DNA and threatens to put tears in my eyes and I want to stuff the whole world inside my heart and keep it there, next to that feeling I get when I read Langston Hughes or when I listen to Sabina or when the creek outside my window tells me to be like it, to carry on regardless of what others are doing and to teach them to fear my wrath.

I hear the cultures that came together to make my blood scream at the fact that no one wanted things to turn out the way they did. I hear them loud and clear in the faces that inhabit my memory, in the voices I carry in my heart, in the color of my skin and the irresistible pull of some spaces, some songs, some poems, some chunks of sand seldom visited by people.

I hear all this and more, and then I open my eyes and read about others wanting "pure blood," wanting to keep their racial purity, their god a blue-eyed hipster, their bastardized language intact. That makes me laugh with closed fists. You don't know the beauty of flavor, pendejo. You keep your dumb ideas of purity and I'll revel in the music of my mixed blood, my mutt blood, my earthly blood, my multitudinous blood, my brown and Rican and black and European and white and African blood, my eternal, magic, ancient blood.

Yeah, when nothing makes sense, I close my eyes and listen to my blood."

Alma stops writing and reads what she wrote. She fixes some typos and changes a few words. She knows it's a strong piece, enough to be yelled at strangers and make them feel something. She also knows it's not enough to make the news. It's not enough to leave a scar on the world, to shake people to their core. To do that, she will need more than words.

LA BRUJA

Outside Piedras Negras, a few miles south of Colonia Venustiano Carranza, lay a few square miles of arid, uninhabited land. The ghost of Inmaculada stood in the middle of that nothingness, whispering bad words that took to the sky like birds of breath looking for weak, angry, hurt souls to invade. They jumped on the backs of words she had already vomited into the night air, words pregnant with hate and hungry for blood. They joined like drops of water running down a surface, finding each other in that same miraculous way loose hairs in a house can find each other and morph into small balls of discarded human.

Inmaculada, almost invisible to the naked eye, was unmoving except for a ghostly tongue that never stopped stirring. Her new form, very much akin to a translucent version of the one she'd had in life, whispered things into the wind so that they would reach ears on both sides of the border. Her anger was boundless. Her thirst for revenge tied her to this side of the veil, and she refused to cross over until enough blood had been spilled to satiate her thirst. Her powers would bring forth death and chaos. Her hechizos would shatter la frontera and poison the fish and make men and women lose their minds until the fire inside her had been extinguished, until enough blood had seeped into the land around her, until the memory of her son was just a tiny star in a universe of screams and suffering. She was ready to stand there and speak into the wind until humanity once again became a forgotten footprint in the sands of time.

Inmaculada's consciousness was somewhere inside that ghost. She could think about what she had turned into, realize that the spirit world tugged at her feet and demanded her presence, but ire and her thirst for revenge had become strong driving forces behind her state, strong enough to keep her between worlds. With the night around her like a cloak and her magic already working, she allowed the memories to come, to once again fill her with purpose.

Everyone in Piedras Negras had been sad to learn their curandera was leaving. Inmaculada didn't want to leave her people behind, including her mother, from whom she still had much to learn, but gang violence had already taken a son from her, and she would not let that happen twice. She refused to feed her own flesh and blood into the hungry beast known as los carteles. La muerte es inevitable, pero se le pueden poner trabas en el camino.

"Vivimos aquí," her husband Rafael often said, "pero la vida está al otro lado del río. Vivir rodeado de muerte no es vivir, es sobrevivir."

Finally, in the middle of the night, a knock had come at their door. They'd packed light, just like the coyote had instructed. With the essential pieces of their life strapped to their backs, they left the home they had built. Inmaculada could sense death in the air, could feel the walls of the house tugging at them as if they'd become magnetized by the years spent inside them, the blood and tears and stories and dreams and moments that happened inside them. She could also smell her family. The fear of her husband and child made their sweat smell like that of unwashed barn animals.

The coyote moved fast, desperately, the way men move when the thing they're trying to escape lives inside them. He spat words at them the way people do when talking to lifelong enemies. His hands lingered on Inmaculada's ass too long as he helped her climb into the back of the truck.

The souls inside were a collection of agony and distress. It was almost too much for Inmaculada. She wanted to clean them all, to bathe them in the river under a full moon and then extract the bad things in their souls with an egg they'd later break against a rock somewhere in the desert. Instead, she had to sit there and try not to cry while looking into the eyes of mothers and fathers that were now in a situation where they felt they had lost their ability to protect their children.

The truck took off. Every sound coming from the vehicle made Inmaculada think they were in the belly of a metallic beast. The truck moved around from side to side, pushing warm bodies against each other. Time constricted and expanded at will. Curves became impossibly long. Heat became a thick monster around them, constant and inevitable. Uncertainty made their hearts beat faster until the primal drum of fear hammered their heads and necks. No one spoke. Concerns were whispered. Fears were confessed into the ears of family members by those who had them and silently voiced to gods by those travelling alone.

Eventually, they came to a stop. All movement stopped, including that of the people. The truck settled. Silence hung in the air like the world holding its breath. The air inside the trailer was heavy with the smell of fear, fried nerves, and blossoming regret. Children whispered and a couple of heavyset individuals breathed hard.

The first hour went by in almost complete silence. No one knew where they were or what was going on outside the doors. The rhythm of fearful waiting, vibrating with the possibility of calamity at its center, overtook everything.

The second hour made them forget the silence. Men who felt the air grow thin knocked on the doors, called on the men who'd driven them there. They did so tentatively at first, like children testing boundaries, and then with anger and desperation. The metal was unyielding and painfully unresponsive.

The third hour brought with it rumors of abandonment. Some folks feared they were in the middle of nowhere, and would remain there until they died. They'd all heard stories like that before, but it wasn't what they were experiencing. It just couldn't be. For a few frantic minutes, almost everyone pounded some part of the truck. Voices rose in volume, became tinged with extreme anxiety. Words like dinero and cabrones and matar flew around like desperate birds, slamming against the inside of the trailer and bouncing around before being drowned by fresh screams. The cacophony scared Inmaculada's son so much he buried his face in her chest and cried the way he cried when the pain was too much to handle como un machito, which is what his father had started telling him to do the second he started walking. The hot, wet air coming from his small mouth was just like the rest of the air around them, and Inmaculada knew that so much heat was a bad thing.

The fourth hour brought La Huesuda to their midst. A woman started wailing, shaking her daughter as if trying to release her from some heat-induced stupor. The tiny body remained lifeless, soft and relaxed in the unalterable way all soulless bodies become once their life force has left them. The mother cried, her tears mixing with the sweat that ran down her face. Some cried with her, for her. Some cried for themselves. Some cried for the meaning of that tiny body. Some just used their shaking hands to wipe away the sweat that kept coming. They felt themselves slide the rest of the way into panic. The heat soon became too much. Bodies that had been pressed against each other for hours now became threats. Everyone looked around then and saw nothing but oxygen thieves making the temperature rise. They were all submerged in a deadly, collective fever, and pushing people away became a reasonable facsimile for aspirin. Cuando la muerte se presenta, cualquier vestigio de humanidad como símbolo de hermanda se desvanece y una sed de sobreviven-cia se presenta, animal e inevitable como un tornado.

The fifth hour was the beginning of the end. The light coming through a few spots in the door announced the arrival of a new day. The temperature kept rising. Every exhalation contributed. Inmaculada couldn't hold her son any longer. The kid was breathing with his mouth open, gulping air so humid and blistering it felt like soup. Then he stopped, and her heart shattered into a million pieces.

The children were the first to go. The men joined in an effort to break the doors down. They made space on the floor and used their legs to kick the doors in unison. When that failed, the biggest ones joined forces and hurled their bodies together at the walls and doors in a bizarre, grotesque ballet. Their flesh bounced off the doors time and again until the futility of their actions became as clear as their doom. They asked the women for help then and tried again, moving as a single body, an entity bent on survival.

None of it worked.

All they managed to do was hurt themselves and increase the heat inside the trailer even more, turning it into a box of hell. Sweat poured off their bodies and made them look like they'd stepped into the shower fully clothed.

There was no space to place the bodies of those who'd already died. They were a hindrance to all who weren't tied to them by blood and love.

Inmaculada couldn't cry. Her anger was bigger than anything she'd ever felt, including her pain. She felt like her skin was peeling off her body. She didn't want to look at her son, his body somewhere on the floor in front of her, being trampled and kicked by desperate people looking for an inch of extra space where there was none. Her husband never came back. The last thing Inmaculada saw was a young boy like her son, his eyes open, his body on top of a man who was probably his father. Both were motionless, pushed against a wall. The father had become his son's deathbed. Inmaculada swore revenge against the men who had done this to them, swore she'd stick around until all the coyotes were dead and there was enough blood along the border to make powerful people take care of the problems that had put them in that trailer. Then she closed her eyes, felt the sweat run down her eyelids like the last caress of her physical being, and stepped into the darkness.

The hours that followed were filled with the loudest silence the desert had ever heard. Even the insects evaded the ominous stillness of the place, and took their calls elsewhere. Birds made wild turns in the sky and changed direction as if they'd crashed against an unseen wall. Then, once darkness had once again descended on the trailer, which did nothing to lower the blistering temperature that cooked the bodies trapped inside, Inmaculada's ghost emerged from the sand next to the truck's rear tires like a bamboo shoot seen in fast-forward. She felt her loss and anger and opened her new mouth. The sound that came from it would be talked about for days. The man who came closest to nailing a description told his wife the next day "Se me pararon todos los vellos del cuerpo, mujer. Pensé que un centenar de coyotes habían agarrado altoparlantes y gritado a la misma vez. Te juro que pensé que el que gritaba era el mismísimo Diablo." However, the man was wrong. It wasn't a hundred coyotes with bullhorns howling at once and it wasn't the Devil himself. The thing that had screamed that night was the soul of a shattered, hurt mother facing the loss of everything she loved, and that is something even the Devil should fear.

PEDRITO

The taxi bounced up and down on shock absorbers that refused to absorb. The rosary hanging from the rearview mirror moved from side to side and up and down like it was suffering an epileptic fit. The taxi driver scowled into the rearview mirror, his face the definition of confused anger. He kept looking at Pedrito with his brows pushed against each other, studying him the way folks study animals they've never seen before and would rather not touch.

The man had picked him up in the city and frowned when Pedrito told him where he wanted to go. "Eso es lejos, mijo, tienes la plata para llegar hasta ahí?" he'd asked. Pedrito had nodded, but the man had kept staring. Then the kid showed him the money. The rest of the time they had both kept silent.

The movie Pedrito had inside his head kept playing on a loop. In it, his father's brains splattered on the dirt a few feet from the river, his blood slowly crawling toward the gaping mouth of a green monster. He could access parts of that day at will, but he kept thinking about that moment, that specific scene with the pink mess plopping out of his father's skull onto the dirt and the gar's teeth shining under the sun a few feet away. The images kept him moving. The trip he was taking was also there, a present and a future that already existed in his brain in the shape of a past. He knew the driver would stop about thirty feet from a dilapidated building, grab the money, and turn back. He knew the man would forget about him in less than 48 hours. These things were clear in his head, as clear as if they had already happened. Pedrito also knew his mom, who cried and passed out three times during the funeral, would keep taking those pills she kept on top of the fridge until they put her in a sleep so deep that her body would forget it had to breathe and pump blood through her system. He knew she was alive back home, probably wondering where he was in between taking her pills, drinking, and passing out, but he also knew her worry wouldn't last long. Her soul had left her body, flying to the river in a dumb quest to bring his father back to life with tears. Pedrito was sad

65

that he would not be there to kiss his mother one last time once the last breath had left her lungs and her body turned into a heavy mass of flesh and bones on top of the dented mattress in her room, but he knew he had to move, he had to be where he was headed.

Señorita Mendoza once told them about déjà vu in class. It's a French word for that odd feeling you get when you feel like you've already seen something or been somewhere. This, however, was different. Pedrito knew exactly what was going to happen, and he didn't feel strange about it. He also knew that what he was going to do would be bad, but, as his abuelo told him more than once, sometimes bad things are right.

The taxi dipped into another hole and the boy's backpack bumped against his thigh. He looked down at it. He knew that this trip meant he would never get to go home again. Home died with his father. Now he was a new person who had to do something else somewhere else, and he felt calm about it. Intellectually, Pedrito understood he should be feeling afraid. He should cry, ask the man to turn around, feel desperate to be back home. There should be an ache inside him to bring his father back from the dead for one last hug, one last story, one last fishing trip. He felt none of that. The inner space where fear should have been was nothing but darkness. All he could see was what lay ahead for him, the pain and the pleasure. All he could feel was the certainty that what he was doing was right and that the ghost of his father, locked in the dirt and thirsty for vengeance, would feed on the blood he'd spill and finally go to heaven to be with his own father.

The taxi turned right into yet another unpaved road and eventually pulled up about thirty feet from a single-story building covered in graffiti. The driver turned around. "Llegamos, mijo, bájese no más."

The kid pulled his backpack onto his shoulder and opened the door. He stepped out of the taxi and inhaled the dry air. It smelled awful. He walked to the driver's side window, shoved his hand in his pocket, pulled out all the money in there, the money he took from the coffee can next to his mother's pills, and handed it all to the man. He knew it was much more than the fare, but the man stuck the crumpled bills in his pockets without a word.

Pedrito turned around and started walking toward the building while sticking his thin arms through the back-pack's straps. Then the voice of the driver reached his ears. He turned. "Ven pa' cá un momento, pinche escuincle." Pedrito ignored the insult and walked toward the man.

"Este es un mal sitio para un chamaco. Agarra mi tarjeta. Si necesitas un taxi de vuelta, me llamas. Aunque no tengas plate. Eso lo arreglamos después, chale?"

Pedrito nodded and grabbed the business card. It was damp with the man's sweat. The driver ran his eyes over him again and reached for the rearview mirror. A moment later, he stuck his hand out the window, the rosary dangling from his finger.

"Toma, ponte esto en el pescuezo. Que la Guadalupana te acompañe."

Pedrito grabbed the rosary. It was warm from all that dancing in the sun. He didn't thank the man, because all he could think about was going inside the building and doing what he knew had to be done.

The driver inhaled deeply and exhaled like a frustrated teacher. Then he put the car in reverse, turned slowly, put it in drive, and drove away. A soft, brown cloud of earthy dust followed the taxi down the unpaved road. Pedrito dropped the rosary on the ground and walked over to the graffiti-covered building. The dark thing inside him pushed him forward. He didn't resist.

THE MOTHER

When the sun was out, the nightmares hid in the cracks on the wall just like the cockroaches. The Mother watched the Boy play by himself in the front of the house and almost managed to forget everything that was wrong. The dishes were waiting for her hands. She hadn't cooked in two days, and there was no more bread or tortas in the house. The laundry was a stinky, multicolored pile near the bathroom door that she hadn't dared to look at in days for fear of what she'd see moving around in there if she did.

She sat at the table. The old wood seemed to be infecting her with its nature. Her joints felt like they were locking up. Her skin felt like it was turning into thin bark. In her head, her bones were becoming branches. Part of her wanted to fight all of it. Another part was just waiting for the creature inside her to make its final exit and for her feet to grow tiny roots that would forever hold her to the ground underneath the table.

The laughter of the Boy was a balm on her soul, but the darkness inside her was more powerful than the laughter. Although there was no hate in her heart, she had somehow come to understand, to understand it the same way she understood that she would give her life for the Boy, that the slimy monster in her womb was a thing born out of hate, a slithering demon thirsty for revenge that had been given flesh by some higher power. Against this knowledge there was nothing. Despair had come and gone in record time. Desperation was a thin layer of muted something boiling under her dried, cracking skin. It felt like she had stopped looking for a solution a few moments before starting to do so. She knew all this, and she knew her inaction stemmed from the fiend that twisted around in her belly. That thing, regardless of its name, had turned her into a vehicle with no willpower.

The Boy's laughter erupted again. A dog's heavy breathing informed the Mother that the Boy was playing with the neighbor's dog.

"Sonríe, mijo," she said to the empty space around her. "Sonríe hoy, mañana y siempre."

THE COYOTE

"No más viajes por unos días," said Clemencia. The coyote thought about asking why, but his fear of the old woman kept his tongue frozen in his mouth like a fat, sleeping slug.

"You want to know why."

It wasn't a question. The woman seemed to be able to read minds. That was part of why the coyote feared her so much. The other part came from the stories he'd heard. She had come to the United States as a teenager, and her mother had found her a job cleaning rooms at a cheap motel somewhere on the outskirts of Dallas. The guy who ran the joint had dealings with the some rednecks who ran the local drug business, providing a hiding space/meeting point for the dope runners. One night, a group of five men coming back from a drop stayed at the hotel. They got drunk. Two of them went out to get more booze and, on their way

71

back, saw Clemencia prepping towels outside the laundry room. They carried her to their room, slung over the biggest one's shoulder like a sack of potatoes. Half an hour later, the place was drowning in red and blue lights. The cops had never seen anything like it. The five men seemed to have been devoured by wolves. Big, angry, incredibly strong wolves that happened to be very hungry. Clemencia never talked about it, but the coyote knew something other than an old lady was hiding behind the soft, crinkled flesh that covered her body.

"Whatever you say goes, jefecita, but I'd like to get more kids across before la migra gets even tighter with that fucking President Pendejo."

"Weird things are happening, mijo. Cosas malas. Huele a sangre ahí afuera. Plus, the orange man is threatening to tighten up security en la frontera. This means that the militias that run up and down there like they own the place will be desperate to get a few more dollars in their pockets before the whole thing collapses under too many eyes and too many government guns, me entiendes?"

Every instinct in the coyote's body was pushing him to argue, to say something. The kids that needed to be transported were already waiting. From what he had been reading in the newspapers, a day could make a difference for them in the current political climate. The time to move was now. Screw waiting around. Still, he kept his mouth shut.

"The important decisions are made by those less affected by them, mijo," said Clemencia. "I love that you are eager to keep doing your job, but taking kids to the frontera now would be like delivering newborn lambs into a cage full of lions."

"Is it men doing bad things? You know I have my gun and…"

"Bad men doing bad things is just part of it, mijo," she said. "I don't have all the details, but I know bad things are going on and it's better to stay away. The orange idiot is just the tip of the iceberg. There are other things happening. They are locking kids up in cages, but there is also something darker going on, something evil that I don't think belongs to this world, mijo. I try to see it clearly but…I don't know, it's not normal. Whatever is happening there smells like blood and bad news."

The coyote's doubts were never spoken, but he knew she could hear them in the silent space between them.

Clemencia took two steps toward el coyote and grabbed his upper arm.

"Escúchame. No lleves más niños hasta que yo te diga. I know my explanations are not enough for you, but you need to trust me. Think about it as the smell of death. When something dies inside or around your house, you know there's something dead even if your eyes don't see it. The stench of death is loud and clear. It is all you need to know, right? This is the same. La Huesuda anda rondando la frontera. Keep the kids away. And stay away yourself. We've been doing this for a long time, and we'll keep doing it as soon as all of this blows over, de acuerdo? We'll find new routes and new people to work with on the other side, but for now we have to stay put."

The coyote tried to keep his composure, but the old lady's fingers were like steel ropes coiling around his biceps with the slow, inevitable crushing power of a machine. He nodded while trying to fill his head with white noise so that Clemencia wouldn't know he had other plans. Outside, just like the last few nights, a few coyotes, many more than usual, started throwing their cries up at the sky. The coyote shivered. Clemencia released his arm. He closed his eyes, thought about La Virgencita, and prayed to her silently.

JAIME

Jaime mashed the key fob and heard a small beep, followed by the click of the door unlocking. He yanked it, threw his gun into the passenger's seat, and shoved the key into the ignition as he slammed the door closed.

The Impala was thirteen years old, but it purred to life like a new car. Jaime put it in drive and stepped on the gas. The sirens got closer. The car lurched forward, and for a second, he was pinned to the seat. That reminded him that Cookie's favorite pastime, other than watching television and smoking, was working on the car. He had injected every one of the 240 ponies under the hood with as much juice as possible, and given the motor every conceivable tweak. The result was the surge of speed Jaime felt when he pressed the accelerator: an explosion of rumbling power that blurred everything around him.

He needed a destination, and San Antonio was not a great choice at the moment, so he decided to visit Guillermo, a man who'd given him a few jobs early on, and someone who would be grateful that Jamie kept his mouth shut and did his time without trying to get out of it by snitching on bigger fish. Maybe Guillermo could get him another car, or knew where he could lay low for a couple of days. He would become a ghost. If society was going to push him into the shadows, he was going to become a shark in those shadows.

The end of Bastrop Street came too quickly. Jaime knew there was a big chance he wouldn't have an opportunity to set foot again on the street in which he had been born and raised in a long time, if ever, but the thought didn't stir any feelings inside him. Alabama Street came up and Jaime's instinct yelled at him to stop, but his brain listened to the approaching sirens and yelled even harder to take an immediate right. The screaming sirens got even closer. He glanced in the rearview mirror and spotted the red and blue lights entering his street. It was an old Lumina, a classic black and white cow. Jaime was momentarily thankful for the shitty cars they gave to cops working the Third Ward. He stepped on the gas again and the Impala peeled away to screech onto and then down Alabama Street.

Whatever was in Jaime's chest turned into a monster that sucked the air out of his lungs. He had the cops coming after him. Aggravated assault. Parole violation without a question. And there was a piece in the car. He was going to get arrested. Then Cookie would say he stole his car. Grand theft auto to sweeten the deal. Plus, he was running from the cops. After the beating he gave Cookie, they would surely treat this as a felony, and running from a felony is as good as slapping a judge and pissing on his robe. Jamie would be back in a cell before really having a chance to process that he had made it out of that hellhole. He could hear the clanging of the door behind him. He could hear Jimmy's ghost whispering to him at night. He could see members of La Eme and the Tango Orejón shanking fuckers left and right for control of every hustle that went on behind prison walls…

Fuck that.

The solution out of this mess evaded Jaime, but something was clear as day in his head: he had to escape. He had to fly away. He had to remain free. This could happen. The opposite was not an option. He knew Houston like no one else. He had a fast car with enough gas and muscle to get him wherever he wanted to go…

Red and blue lights splashed across his rearview mirror. They weren't coming from the Lumina. The new car on his tail was something compact and powerful. Probably one of those Chargers he'd seen once or twice, closer to the ground and sliding through the hood at night like a hungry cat stalking its prey. It could move. Jaime stomped on the gas again and the car jumped forward, devouring Alabama Street the way hungry dogs devour fresh meat.

Where could he go? He was hauling ass east on Alabama. He could get on I-45 and gun it. The cops would let him go after a while, right? Probably not. He could put some serious miles between them. If he exchanged cars somewhere after that, he'd be good. All he needed to do was survive the next couple of minutes and he'd be in the clear. There were places to hide. He knew people. Some of them owed him favors. It'd all be fine if he could paddle his way out of shit's creek quickly.

Jaime's eyes darted between the road ahead and the lights in his rearview. The pigs were still behind him. The siren shrieked like an angry banshee. The Impala's engine roared. Jaime kept grinding down on the accelerator, every muscle in his body as tense as a guitar string.

The fucking Charger was gaining. Jaime looked at the approaching lights and thought about long, sad nights in an uncomfortable bed. Assholes kicking their doors and screaming and crying after the lights went off. He thought about those awful shoes and the 90 days he had to do in ad seg for fighting. No calls. No commissary. No visits. Locked down for 23 hours every damn day, loneliness and silence before him like an endless field where nothing grew. He thought about awful meals and shakedowns and the sense that any day could be the day a shank ventilated his insides. He thought about the showers and the screaming and the fear and the constant structure and about hearing rumors about kites containing names and instructions concerning other men whose lives were as worthless as his. He thought about those things and knew he couldn't go back. Not now. Not ever. He returned his eyes to the road and a light brown thing appeared out of Sampson Street. A car. Large. Four doors. Jaime jerked the wheel to the right and the entire world went off-kilter as his body slammed against the door.

For a second there was nothing but the empty pit at the bottom of his stomach as the car turned, fighting gravity and inertia every inch of the way. Two wheels on the asphalt, two wheels in the air. Los pies en el barrio y el grito en el cielo. The world went askew and threatened to stay that way. Jaime's stomach swallowed his nerves and pulled his balls into his abdomen. Then came the sound of the Impala slamming against the car sideways and then grazing its side as it pulled away from it. It was a faster, louder, more metallic version of the end of the world, but the car continued. Nothing exploded. No wobbling from a blown tire. No smoke came from underneath the hood. Jaime inhaled, told himself to keep his eyes on the road in front of him. A second later, he looked at the rearview mirror again. The Charger was still closing in. And it had company.

The Impala screamed into the Alabama-Scott intersection. Jaime braced for an impact that never came. Instead, he pulled the car back under control. One step closer to the interstate. One step closer to freedom. There was nothing but speed in his immediate future, and Jaime smiled at the thought.

The ponies under the car's hood growled as Jaime gunned it across the Elgin Street without a hitch. He knew he would be able to go even faster once he got on the interstate, and that idea almost made him smile again.

A patrol car popped out of Drew Street and blocked Jaime. Panic exploded in his chest as he slammed on the brakes. The Impala protested the change, the tires shrieking against the road. The motor barked, objecting to being asked to do too much. Jaime pulled the wheel to the left and pressed the accelerator again. The vehicle pounced like a desperate animal. He saw people. A brick wall. He clomped on the brakes again and inertia became his worst enemy. His gun flew off the passenger seat and thunked on the floor. He'd done too much too fast, and the car wasn't in the mood. It spun. Horns blared. People screamed. The car made noises it wasn't supposed to make.

Two loops later, he found himself sitting across Scott Street and looking at the entrance to Tuam Street. He needed to get in there and vanish. But he couldn't. Coming toward him was yet another cop car. Jaime smashed his open hand against the steering wheel three times and abandoned the last shards of common sense.

He floored the gas. The Impala roared and lurched forward. Four seconds later, it became obvious the cop wasn't going to move. Jaime mashed the brakes again, yanked the steering wheel, slid in a half-circle. The other two cop cars were waiting for him further down the street.

Jaime leaned on the wheel. He took a deep breath and allowed all the darkness in the universe to enter his soul. His hope of escaping was leaving his body like blood from a slashed artery. He was trapped. There was nowhere else to go now. All escape routes were blocked. With all the people out there, cops would shoot first and never ask questions. Maybe he could ditch the car and run through...

"Come out of the vehicle slowly with your hands above your head! I repeat, come out of the vehicle slowly with your hands above your head!"

Two seconds here and the cops were already giving him orders. Jaime was tired of orders. He was tired of eating when they told him to and showering when they told him to and going to bed when they told him to. He was not going back to any of that shit.

The cop with the bullhorn kept talking. Jaime didn't pay attention to him. Whatever he was saying was inconsequential. Plus, they had left the sirens on.

The red and blue lights were dancing all around him, but he refused to look up. He refused to accept that he was so far up shit's creek that he couldn't see dry land in any direction. And he had lost his paddles. And there was a giant hole in the boat.

The guy with the bullhorn took a second to drink some water. Jaime knew what was coming next. Words that meant nothing. Instructions and pleading. Instead, he listened to the sirens in the distance. More pigs that were coming for him. He hated them all. Then the sound of those sirens shifted and he thought they were angels weeping because he hadn't run fast enough. Angels weeping for another barrio boy caught in all the bullshit. Angels weeping for lost kids and parents thrown in prison. Angels weeping about cops just like the ones surrounding him being too trigger-happy. The ángeles were telling him what he already knew: in order to escape he would have had to have been faster than the red and blue weeping angels. Jaime knew that was impossible now.

Jaime studied the patrol cars on both sides and the way out of the situation hit him. It was a solution that would keep him out of a cell. He would stay away from the fear and the anger and the guns and the drugs and the blood and even the damn cars and gasoline and women and wild nights. He thought about freedom—true freedom—often, and that sealed the deal. Freedom or death, and nothing would stand in his way. He knew he could hitch a ride to a better place on the back of those weeping angels he couldn't beat in a race, so he bent down, grabbed the gun from the floor in front of the passenger's seat, and opened the door.

ALMA

Alma sat up in bed. Her hair was pasted to her forehead. She felt dampness on the back of her neck. Her large t-shirt stuck to her arms uncomfortably, slightly pulling at her shoulders like some half-forgotten thing she had to take care of. This time, the nightmare had been too real.

She had been in a small salon. The lights had shifted from the stage she had been standing on to the large crowd in front of her. A hooded figure had walked onto the stage and given her a very large gun. She had instinctively known who the people in the audience were; gun lobbyists and gun fanatics. Now, awake, she blamed the dream on the incessant debate about gun control she saw on social media every day. "If you won't change things, then things will change you," she had said in her best performance voice. Then she had turned the gun on the crowd and opened fire.

Death. Blood. Falling bodies. Chaos. Then calm. Silence. Then came regret. She had become part of the problem. She had allowed her passion to lead her into a solution that was not what it seemed to be. She had been fooled by her own feelings. Death was not the answer. Her message was dead, drowned in the blood of those who had thought differently. Discourse had become violence, thus ending its status as something that could be discussed. She had killed the people she hated by becoming a killer, which she also hated.

Waking up felt like a merciful change. Her brain moved forward in all directions at once. Her thoughts were wild horses on a slope covered in loose gravel.

She took a deep breath, looked around. Her phone was on the floor, charging. It looked like a grey slug with a long white tail. The dead spermatozoid of the future she'd been promised by technology. She focused on it for a few seconds. She analyzed its shape and the distance between her and the apparatus. She thought about getting on Instagram and recording a short video in her state; sweaty and breathing heavy, her head fuzzy with too many thoughts. Then she thought better of it. It was late. No one would see it. Her post would sink into the black abyss of social media darkness. For an artist, death, she knew, was better than living in oblivion.

There was something unfair about the way society saw art, something that had always bothered Alma. On one hand, she had to be edgy and profound and incredibly smart. On the other hand, she had been told many times that she had to entertain the crowd and make them feel like they were witnessing something special, like they were part of that thing. She also had to provide the right content at the right time in the right platform within the right context. That was all bullshit. She knew her only real job was creating something that hadn't existed until the moment she brought it to life. She loved art, but loathed when art was pushed into the realm of discourse and funneled through digital platforms. If she created a performance, there was something new in the world, something that hopefully spoke to those who experienced it in some way. The plethora of comments, opinions, critiques, and applause around that piece of art were inconsequential. Yeah, she knew all these things, but she also craved attention, recognition, success, money, and the freedom that came with being famous. She wanted to hide away in a cave forever... but also to go viral and travel the world with her art.

Alma got out of bed with a tired grunt and stumbled her way to the kitchen. She opened the fridge. The severed head of a mustachioed man stared back at her with one brown, bloodshot eye and one empty, dark eye socket filled with a pulpy red mess. Alma screamed and looked away while jumping back. Her eyes went back to the fridge. The door was closing. The head wasn't there.

Whatever was going on inside her head would lead to a truly outstanding performance, or would land her in a psychiatric hospital. At the moment, neither option appeared superior to the other.

Alma opened the fridge again and grabbed the pitcher of water from the top shelf, poured herself a glass, and took a big gulp. The taste of copper, the strong odor, and the thick, viscous nature of the water hit her simultaneously. She spat out the contents, gagged, and spit again. She looked down at the glass in her hand. What had been cold water a few seconds ago was now congealing blood.

That's when Alma heard the giggling coming from the closet.

LA BRUJA

Time moved forward at breakneck speed, stopped, and then refused to move forward again. The fabric of reality, such an obvious thing to her even after becoming a ghost, was now a slippery fish whose powerful body Inmaculada couldn't properly grasp.

The anger still burned at her core, and that kept her going. There were many minds she had been able to invade. She could feel it. Her words were doing their job. She didn't know who they were invading or how, but there was an energy coming back to her, an echo of the things that hadn't happened yet, that felt to her like a promise of mayhem. She felt the anger reflecting inside her. She felt the hatred building, buzzing like an angry hive that'd been kicked into action.

Her magia was always strong, but in death it had become unstoppable.

Ella era una diosa nacida de las venas abiertas de los dioses muertos.

She was a rhizomatic entity for whom distance was not an issue, and corporeality unnecessary.

She was an invisible monster made up of angry ghost limbs scattered across the land and hungry for sacrifices.

She was the embryonic tale of sorrow at the center of the universe.

She was the cloistral silence before the explosion, the gasp that precedes a last scream.

She was an avenging angel whose wings had been burned by the flames of retaliation and loathing.

Ella era la energía de la luna y la fuerza de la lluvia envueltas en dolor, falta de paz y sed de venganza.

She was a sacred magnifying glass under the sun of injustice, ready to punish a world full of people who only care about the things that should be ignored.

She was a goddess standing on the dividing line between right and wrong, her head among the angels and her tired feet bathed in the blood of innocents.

She was a saint in the making, the Mother of Chaos, the blood of generations that has been spilled on every forgotten chunk of land across a world where suffering es el pan nuestro de cada dia.

She was the possibility of change and balance.

Ella era todo y nada, el principio y el fin, en ángel de la muerte y la afilada guadaña de la Santa Muerte.

Hovering a few inches over the hot sand, Inmaculada flexed the nonphysical things that had replaced her muscles and felt their power. She screamed. Animals screamed with her. The land shook. Vengeance was her obedient dog. Magic was her weapon. Blood was her fuel.

PEDRITO

The house looked uninhabited. The windows were boarded up and the paint looked like it had started needing a new coat two decades and many rainy days ago. Pedrito forgot everything about the taxi driver and started walking toward the left side of the building.

There were two options: knock on the door or walk around and try to get a sense of the place before coming face to face with the man he had come looking for. The first option would probably lead to a bullet to the head or just silence. The second, Pedrito knew, would probably get him closer to the man he needed to see. How he knew this was a mystery, but there was the movie in his head, always guiding him now, showing him a sliver of the future. Also, walking for a bit around the place would satisfy his curiosity. He had been to cemeteries at night and even gone up to the door of the town's best-known bruja, Doña Marina, but this was different. This was the place the newspapers called La Casa de la Muerte. This place was so packed with ghosts Pedrito was surprised he hadn't seen an apparition yet.

As Pedrito walked around the building, the smell of death came to him. It crawled into his nose and made him gag. It was sweet and pungent at the same time. He had smelled dead things before, a rat here, a run-over dog there, but this was different. This felt like a version of that smell that had been tampered with. It was at once organic and chemical, like a dead dog festering in the midday sun while covered in the cleaning products Pedrito's mom used in the bathroom. He stopped walking. He closed his eyes and inhaled the putrid scent. It wasn't that bad. It reminded him of his father, who had only smelled like blood and feces at the end. He could almost taste the sweetness in the air in the back of this throat. He opened his eyes and kept walking.

The man he had come to see, Santiago Santos, was known around Mexico as El Cocinero, the stewmaker. Pedrito had learned everything about him after his father had left a newspaper on top of the kitchen table that contained an article about the man. His job, according to the piece, was as easy as it was horrific: to turn the bodies the carteles brought him into unrecognizable puddles of goo by dissolving them in lye. The carteles used him to take care of the bodies of people who, for one reason or another, had to disappear completely. As a result of his job, people feared him. "Ese baila con la Huesuda." That's what some guy interviewed by the newspaper had said. He dances with death. Pedrito had read that the carteles only dropped bodies there during the day because no one wanted to go there at night. If the carteles were afraid of him, then everyone had to be afraid of him. Very afraid. Even the police were too scared to come looking for him and, according to Pedrito's father, accepted money, a mordida, to stay away from his place and let him do his grisly business in peace. Pedrito didn't care about any of that. His father had left that newspaper article on Santos a few months ago and Pedrito had been thinking about the man ever since. The article said he knew everything that went on along la frontera, and that was a place Pedrito cared about deeply. La frontera held his dreams. It was the promise his father made to him regularly. It was the path to a new life, el camino a un futuro mejor. On top of that, the article on Santos ended with a paragraph on how the man had also become a key player in keeping the rogue gringo militias under control. In other words, he walked hand in hand with La Santa Muerte and controlled la frontera with her power. Pedrito believed all of it. He had come looking for him because of that.

The dilapidated building had a gate on the west side. It was covered by chunks of zinc and wood. A heavy chain with a massive rusted lock hanging from it kept the gate closed. As he approached the gate, the smell of death intensified.

Pedrito reached the front of the gate and tried to peek through the cracks and holes in the plywood. Only glimpses came at him. Dirt. Pieces of wood on the floor. A dirty sliver of wall splattered with dirt thrown up by the last rain. He stepped closer and bent over a bit to place his right eye over one of the holes. There were no plants on the other side. It was supposed to be a garden, but it looked more like a construction site. There were strange rectangular pits in the dirt. White buckets littered the ground. Suddenly a black thing appeared and lunged at his right eye, all teeth and speed. The body on the other side of the plywood slammed against it so hard the whole thing moved, smacking Pedrito's forehead and pushing him back. He lost his balance and landed on his ass. The dry ground around him puffed a sigh of thin dirt and a few pebbles dung into the palms of his hands. He scurried back, fearing the dog on the other side would tear the whole thing down and come

94

at his throat at any second. The piece of plywood held. The beast barked. It was a throaty, wet, snarling sound that felt like all the anger in the world was packed tight inside the dog's body.

Pedrito stood up and dusted his pants off. He checked his hands. There were tiny indentations where the pebbles had dug into his skin, but none had been sharp enough to draw blood. He looked up at the post-apocalyptic setup in front of him and remembered a few scenes from movies that took place in a world where clean things no longer existed. He now understood that world had always been real, had always existed under what everyone considered normal, and now that he was on his own, the ugly parts were all he could see.

With the dog already aware of his presence, there was no use in sneaking around, so Pedrito walked back to the door he had seen before and knocked on it. The silence on the other side of the door struck him as forced, pregnant with something tense, something that belonged to the world of screams, but that was forced to stay quiet.

Click.

The sound was metallic. Loud and clear. Too clear to have come from deep inside the house. Then Pedrito heard a shoe scrape against something. The sound came from somewhere above his head. He looked up. A skinny man with black pants, a black shirt, and very brown, sweaty skin was holding a massive rifle in front of his face. The barrel of the cannon was pointing at Pedrito's face.

"¿Quién eres y qué quieres?"

The man's voice was calm. He was asking questions, but he didn't sound curious. Pedrito knew no bullet would fly out of that gun, at least not while it was pointed at his face. The movie in his head didn't show him dying at this door.

"Me llamo Pedro. Quiero hablar con Santos."

"¿Qué quieres con Santos? ¿Andas solo?"

"Si, ando solo. Quiero trabajar con Santos."

The man chuckled. The door opened. Pedrito's heart jumped in his chest. He lowered his eyes. The rectangle behind the door was too dark for his sun-blasted pupils. He only saw the silhouette of a figure standing there. A gun flew up at him like a metallic fish jumping out of a lake of shadows. The barrel tapped against his forehead. The hand holding the gun lifted a thumb and clicked the hammer at the back of the gun. Pedrito kept quiet.

Santos stepped out of the dark and looked around, the gun trained on Pedrito's face. Then he grabbed Pedrito's arm and yanked him inside the house.

The door slammed behind them. Santos' face was next to his. The gun remained pressed against his forehead, just above his left eyebrow. The man's breath was worse than the smell outside. Heat was coming off of him like a bad fever. His tanned face was covered with patches of new beard that had been neglected for a week or so. Yellow, black, and brown mixed in his mouth, but Pedrito didn't focus long enough to figure out which color belonged to what.

"A la casa del Diablo no viene nadie que no venga a dejar dinero o un cuerpo. La única otra opción es venir aquí a morir. ¿Tú a qué a carajo viniste, pinche niño?"

Pedrito was nervous. He felt like someone was pulling his chin down toward his neck while simultaneously keeping his mouth shut. He swallowed, remembered his father's brain splattering on the dirt next to the gaping fish, and spoke.

"Tu matas milicianos gringos en la frontera. Lo leí en el periódico. A mi papá lo mató un pinche miliciano. Ahora quiero matar unos cuantos yo para vengar a mi papá."

Pedrito's voice didn't crack. It didn't waiver or stop. Santos lowered the gun as he ran his hand over Pedrito's waist, the back of his shirt, and then the inside of his legs all the way to his testicles. Pedrito flinched, instinctively tiptoed. Santos stood up straight and placed the gun in the back of his pants.

Just like the dog, Pedrito wasn't expecting the slap Santos gave him. His hand flew out of nowhere and struck him low on the left side of his face. He felt his jaw twist sideways and then the back of his head smacked against the floor. Everything went dark for a couple of seconds. His body wanted him to do something, but all he managed to do was tense every muscle and lift his arms off the floor. Santos jumped on top of him, straddled him, and grabbed his wrists and pulled them to the center of his chest.

Santos brought his face close to Pedrito's face once again and spoke in a low, angry voice.

"Esta es la Casa de la Muerte, pinche enano. I don't know who sent you, but I don't like this game. Nadie quiere trabajar conmigo así porque si. Mucho menos un enano de mierda como tu. Me vas a decir quién te envió ahora mismo o te voy a matar sin dejarte levantar del pinche suelo. So tell me who sent you. Was it the gringos?"

His breath was smacking Pedrito harder than the slap. It was like week-old roadkill floating in booze. It stung the youngster's nose and made his eyes water.

"No one sent me. I want to kill milicianos. Te lo juro por la Virgencita."

Santos' hand moved again, as quickly as it had moved when he slapped Pedrito. The sharp tip of a knife dug into the skin underneath Pedrito's chin. Santos pressed the knife a bit. It was so sharp, the tip popped the kid's skin and sank into his flesh. Screaming would mean stabbing himself even more, impaling his lower jaw, so Pedrito kept his mouth shut. He knew he wasn't going to die there. His death wasn't clear, but it wasn't here, and it wasn't tied to Santos' hands, to this moment, to this knife under his chin. The visions had shown him that much.

There were footsteps behind Santos. The man turned toward the sound.

"Este pinche hijueputa tiene los nervios de acero o está más loco que una cabra," the stewmaker said to the man from the roof.

Santos stood up. He offered Pedrito a hand and pulled him up to his feet.

"Let me get this straight, kid: you're here because you want to kill milicianos? Viniste hasta aquí, hasta la boca del lobo, sólo porque quieres vengar a tu padre?"

"Si."

"Have you ever killed anything before?"

Pedrito thought about insects and fish and knew that, even though *yes* was not the answer the man was expecting, it was the right answer to give.

"Si. He matado…y he visto a la muerte de cerca."

99

Santos grabbed him by the arm again and dragged him away from the door and deeper into the house.

Santos kept walking, quietly pulling Pedrito down a hallway that opened into an empty room and then through a door that lead outside. The kid realized he was standing in the spot that he had been trying to look at a few minutes ago. The dog was nowhere to be seen. Santos kept jerking him forward.

Santos stopped in front of one of the rectangular pits. He let go of Pedrito's now sore arm. The man walked a few steps to a wall and grabbed a long stick that had once belonged to a broom.

"Mira," said the stewmaker as he stuck the stick into the hole.

Pedrito looked inside the hole. A thick, smelly, milky substance filled the pit a third of the way. Santos began moving it around with the stick. The smell worsened, coming up to the kid's nose like an angry animal and burrowing into his nose and the back of his throat. Chunks of whatever the hell was in there popped to the surface before disappearing back into the milky stew once again.

"Aquí hay dos cuerpos," said Santos. "Huesos. Piel. Pelo. De todo. Dos personas. Dos pinches muertos. This is why they called this the house of death, kid. Esos barriles

100

de allá son para echar lo que quede después. I can put ten or twelve bodies in each barrel. Haha. You sure you want to work with me? This is what I do. Every single fucking day. Yo soy el cocinero de la muerte. Yo soy Dios y el Diablo aquí. Yo soy el fin."

The kid paid attention to what he was seeing. He thought he recognized a finger. Then Santos turned the stick sideways and started poking around, lifting it out of the mess every few seconds and making the smell even worse with each move. A few seconds later, he pulled it up. A human skull was at the end of the stick, which went through the left eye socket. There were strips of skin still attached to it. There was also what seemed to Pedrito like half a mustache attached to the skull. The milky substance dripped from the teeth like the thing was salivating. It reminded Pedrito of zombie movies.

"¿Tienes ganas de vomitar?"

Pedrito was far from comfortable, but none of what he was seeing and smelling was making him nauseous. These were pits full of decaying bodies. The people that had once inhabited these bodies were no longer around. They were in heaven or in hell, depending on how they had behaved. If they had been bad, then they were burning in hell. If they had been good people, maybe they were in heaven with his father, la Virgencita and el Niño Jesús. Pedrito decided that, if they had ended up in el cocinero's house, they were probably not good people, and that made him care even less.

"No, I don't want to throw up."

Santos smiled at him, nodding. He dropped the skull back into the milky stew with a plop, shook the stick, walked back to the wall, and returned it to the spot against the wall from which he had grabbed it.

"Ven conmingo."

This time, Santos did not pull on his arm. That was a welcome change. Pedrito followed him, first back across the garden, noticing the dozens of holes in the ground, and then into the darkness of the house.

They walked back through the hallway and entered another part of the house. Pedrito saw there was no furniture except for a large sofa under a window and a small fridge next to it. Santos walked halfway down hallway and opened a door on the left. The smell that escaped the room was like a wall of pestilence that crashed against Pedrito's face and sent him back a few steps. The stench was so potent it seemed to wrap its fingers around his throat and squeeze the life out of him, preventing him from breathing. He coughed twice, feeling his saliva get thick and slippery, the way it did when he had a cold or drank something cold after playing out in the sun for a while.

Pedrito pushed against the stench and entered the room.

Santos was standing next to two bodies. Two men. They were naked, pressed against the wall. One was face down. The kid looked at the man's arms, which were stuck beneath him, and wondered if they were tied together. Then he looked at the dark holes that covered his back in a gory polkadot pattern. Flies buzzed around each black hole. The man's back wasn't covered in blood, so maybe someone had already done something to the body.

The second man was face up, his arms raised over his head like a kid on a rollercoaster. His belly was huge. Pedrito looked at where his penis should be and couldn't see it. Between the belly and the black hair down there, it was impossible. Maybe they had cut it off. Pedrito looked at his face. There was a single hole between his eyes. There were no teeth in his open mouth and his torso was covered with purple bruises and peppered with tiny red welts that looked like infected mosquito bites.

Santos took a step toward him. Pedrito looked at Santos. Something strange shone in the middle of his bloodshot eyes. Santos was holding his gun out, the barrel pointed at himself instead of at Pedrito's head this time.

"¿Sabes cómo usar una pistola, escuincle?"

Pedrito shook his head. Santos turned his body, grabbed his gun with both hands, and told him what to do. Then he handed the gun to him again. Pedrito grabbed it. It was much heavier that he expected. And it was cooler, too, as if the metal was cursed and the heat was afraid to get too close to it.

"See that guy with the bullet hole in his head? Mátalo otra vez. Lléna a ese cabrón de plomo."

The kid grabbed the gun. He didn't understand why el cocinero was asking him to shoot a man who was already dead, but he was going to do it anyway. He stepped closer to the body, wrapped both hands around the piece, aimed with one eye closed, and squeezed the trigger.

The blast deafened him. The gun pushed his arms back so hard it bent his elbows and came within an inch of striking him in the face. The bullet went into the head of the dead man, right above his ear. The head shook a bit. Dark liquid trickled out of the hole. He heard a bicycle ringer in his head. Pedrito looked at Santos. The stewmaker was smiling. His teeth were a yellowish mess of stumps under cracked lips. The kid lowered the gun.

The guy from the roof ran into the room, the weapon exactly where it had been when he was threatening to rain death on top of Pedrito.

"Relájate, pendejo," said Santos, bringing his hand up to stop the man from doing whatever it was he thought the man was about to do. "Estaba probando al enano. Parece que va en serio el cabroncito. Tiene los cojones bien puestos."

The man in black lowered his weapon. He looked at Pedrito and then at Santos again. His face looked like he was trying to figure out a math problem.

"Oye, escuincle, dispararle a un muerto es fácil. Un cuerpo sin alma asusta menos que arráncarle el alma a uno llenito de vida. ¿Que harías si te dijera que le dispares a Mateo?" Santos asked, jutting his chin out toward the confused man in front of them.

Pedrito lifted the gun again, his left eye already closed, aimed for a second, and squeezed the trigger. Mateo's black shirt puffed up like a flag caught in a sudden gust of wind and he took a step back. Mateo reached up to the hole in his chest, but his hands never made it. He collapsed forward, first to his knees and then on top of his gun. The ringing in Pedrito's ears got worse, but he heard a loud explosion of laughter coming from behind him. The sound was like someone laughing through a wet towel. He turned around. Santos was bent over, smacking his hand against his filthy jeans as if the body on the floor was the most hilarious thing he had ever seen. He was still laughing when Pedrito approached him and gave him his gun back.

THE MOTHER

Death. That was the only option. It was everywhere. Death took her husband. Death lived inside her. Death was coming out at night, preying on children throughout the town. The Mother had heard the rumors already. Parents finding their babies dead in their cradles, their tiny bodies devoured by some animal. Blood everywhere. Slithering trails of blood left on floors and windowsills. She felt responsible.

Did she have what it took to wait for the monster, to kill it? Maybe. Would she be able to? She didn't know. The thing was an alien, a parasite, a monster, a nightmare made flesh, but it was still her baby. It was still the last thing that her husband had given her. A baby to take care of. Maybe that's exactly what she needed. Maybe a brother was what The Boy needed to forget their bad luck, to keep him from realizing just how poor they were.

No. The thing inside her could not be allowed to continue living, to continue killing. She had to do something, and she had to do it soon.

The mere thought of action tired her. Thinking about the physical aspect of killing the sliding horror in her womb made her want to take a nap.

She was sitting on the small kitchen table. The Boy was outside. She could hear him in the distance, screaming and laughing with his friends, oblivious to the nightmare going on under his own roof, of the awful creature that was born every damn night in the same room where he slept.

The heat was oppressive. The Mother wanted a glass of cold water, but getting up from the table seemed impossible. She was too tired. And she was somehow becoming one with the table. That was impossible, but it was happening. It had been happening for a while. Her body would get stuck to things if she stayed in contact with them for too long. It took her a long time to pull her body free of the mattress every morning. If she sat on the toilet for too long, her skin would stick to the white surface. Whenever she sat at the kitchen table, her ass and elbows begged to remain glued to the chair and table.

She also felt her joints stiffening. This was something she wanted to attribute to the pregnancy, but couldn't. It felt too wrong, too surreal. It had started a few days before, and now if she sat for too long, her knees would crack loudly when she finally stood up. It was painful. The idea of seeing a doctor crossed her mind, but she had no money and no insurance. And she didn't want anyone to know about the thing she was carrying. What would they do if they knew the thing that had been killing and eating babies was her own…she couldn't think of it as a child, but it definitely felt like hers.

Sitting at that table, the skin of her elbows and forearms almost unperceptively melting into the old, scratched wood, The Mother had a breakthrough. She suddenly understood what was happening. She saw everything clearly. The creature. The hardening of the joints and subsequent loss of mobility. The sense of being where she was but simultaneously away from her body. The constant tiredness. Her inability to move much when the monster was leaving her insides. She understood it all. She was becoming a human cocoon.

Tears fell from her eyes and splattered quietly onto the table and the top of her arms. The salty liquid ran down her cheeks and tickled her neck.

The Boy's laughter came at her again. He was closer to the house now. Probably hungry. The more he played, the hungrier he got. He depended on her for most things. The feeling behind the tears shifted. Fear and sadness vanished. Anger and love flourished, overtook everything, and shoved air into her lungs. She shivered and pulled an arm off the table. Pieces of skin remained, glued to the wood. She wiped away the tears. She would not become a human cocoon. Her life belonged to The Boy. She couldn't leave him alone in a world that already taken his father from him. She was going to kill the monster in her womb the next time it came out. She was going to kill that fucking thing, or die trying.

THE COYOTE

The coyote had a dream. In it, he saw a small house in the middle of nowhere. Darkness surrounded it like an oppressive force. No light shone in the distance. No insects chirped or crawled around it. The only presence was that of the light pouring out of a window and the bulb above the entrance door and the sound of crying children.

The coyote could see everything, but when he looked down, he realized he had no body. He ached for the children inside that house. The pain in them was almost palpable. He wanted to do something, to grow a physical body and run to help them, to pull them away from whatever evil was making them cry in that awful, desperate way. He approached the window without fear, understanding he was invisible, powerless, and looked inside. A young girl was standing against a wall. Two men were throwing beer caps at her. They were plucking them from a table where they sat, which was covered in empty beer bottles, caps, napkins, empty food containers, and other assorted garbage.

The girl was whimpering, screaming only whenever a bottle cap struck her skin. The coyote was sure the screaming had to do more with nerves than pain, but he still wanted to kill those men more than anything. Next to the girl, a little boy stood in nothing but diapers. His tiny body was covered in red welts, and a large purple bruise took up almost half of the right side of his face. On that side, the eye was closed like that of a boxer who'd just taken a beating. His eyes were glued to a spot on the wall. Tears ran down his face, but he wasn't trying to run away.

Something broke inside the coyote's chest. He felt like crying, but couldn't. He wanted to run in there and save those kids, but he had no feet. He also lacked arms to dish out punishment, or hands with which to hold a gun.

A sound akin to wind howling through a deserted street engulfed the coyote. At first he thought it was an airplane or some other large, airborne vehicle tearing the night sky in half over the house. He looked up, searching for the source of the deafening sound, but there was nothing above him. He looked to the right and saw nothing. Then he looked to the left. A ball of blinding white light was approaching. It moved faster than any airplane. A second later, the light consumed everything, the noise becoming a wall of unstoppable sound that prevented any action. Then it all fizzled away.

A figure appeared. Ten feet from where the coyote stood, the light collapsed onto itself to reveal a humanoid form. As the light retreated, it became clear that it was a woman. She had on a long white veil. Underneath that, the coyote saw a red dress that shimmered and flowed down her body. It was a dress made of blood. Around her shoulders, the woman wore a blue sash.

The coyote immediately knew who he was looking at. He had seen the same image stare at him from his own walls, a thousand candles throughout his lifetime, and the pearl grips of his Sig Saur 1911. It was La Virgencita. La sagrada Madre de Dios. Her tanned face stood in stark contrast to the white veil. She was darker than the depictions in his shirts, paintings, and candles, but her face was the same. Simple. Calm. Gorgeous. It inspired peace. It made him feel at ease. It filled him with joy. The coyote wanted to drop to his knees, to start praying to the holy vision before him, but his lack of a body prevented all of it. Instead, he took in the glorious figure, the edge of lights around her body, the outstretched palms radiating a strange, visible warmth that shimmered in the air, the blood perennially running down her form, but never reaching the floor.

Before the coyote could do anything, La Virgencita moved. She approached the house without moving her sandaled feet. When she reached the door, she lifted her right hand and placed it against the wrecked wood. The door imploded into the house with so much force it slammed against the opposite wall.

The two men who had been torturing the kids jumped to their feet. Their jaws hung open. Their eyes bulged out. Their hands trembled. Confusion knotted their features into spastic masks of fear.

One of them started kneeling, his mouth moving in what surely was an apology or a desperate prayer, but La Virgencita moved. She brought her arms behind her back and then back to the front again. Two Sig Sauers 1911, just like the one the coyote carried around. The coyote knew this Virgencita was the one in his own gun's pearl grips, and she was here to do the same thing he tried to do: she was going to rain down justice across la frontera.

The coyote looked on as La Virgencita closed her eyes and pulled both triggers at once. The guns spit bullets that left a trail of light behind them. They struck the men between the eyes. White light poured from the holes as if their skulls contained a powerful flashlight instead of a brain. They opened their mouths. More light came out. They started shaking. Light came from their ears and eyes. The tips of their fingers started emitting light as well, tenuous at first but quickly growing into the same blinding whiteness that had shone outside before la Virgencita showed up.

As the men vanished into the light, surely on their way to the eternal punishment they deserved, La Virgencita approached the children. She touched the girl's face and the marks on her skin vanished. Her face became clean. She stopped crying and shivering. A smile pulled her lips up as her eyes filled with tears of joy. "Madrecita," said the girl, a single, powerful world that contained a universe of gratitude and a lifetime of recognition. Then La Virgencita moved to the side and touched the boy's right cheek. The bruise disappeared. The swelling in his eye sucked back into his body and his eye appeared, healthy and shiny as it looked up at the mother of God standing in front of him.

La Virgencita then turned around and looked straight at the coyote. For a second he feared for his life. The vast array of peccadilloes he had committed danced in his memory. Every lie. Everything he had stolen since he was a child. Every act of violence. Every drop of blood spilled into the unforgiving desert. Every night spent on a stained mattress over and under a woman he would never love. Every explosion of anger. Every selfish moment. Every single time he had looked up at the unresponsive sky and doubted his own faith, doubted God himself as the bodies piled up and the horror stories kept on repeating themselves and the frontera seemed oblivious to the pain and the hustle and the damaged flesh and the abandoned kids.

He expected the guns to fly back up and spit deadly light his way at any second. Instead, an overwhelming peace came over the coyote, with the power of intravenous morphine. He understood that those things would not be punished. In the balance of the soul, he was a good man. There were other things, more serious things, to take care of. La Virgencita knew where he stood, and in her beautiful eyes he read the silent message she was sending him: *Go forth, my soldier, and make right all that which has been made wrong by the hands of evil men.*

Now, on his way to see Father Frank, the coyote felt a new strength inside him. There was a divine force pushing him forward, telling him that all that needed to be done was okay in the eyes of God because la Virgencita had sent him on a special mission, a holy mission. Si la frontera estaba sucia, el sería la luz divina encargada de limpiarla.

The coyote drove on, intoning his favorite prayer like a mantra:

Dios te salve, María, llena eres de gracia, el Señor es contigo.

Bendita tú eres entre todas las mujeres, y bendito es el fruto de tu vientre, Jesús.

Santa María, Madre de Dios, ruega por nosotros, pecadores, ahora y en la hora de nuestra muerte.

Amén.

JAIME

The cop with the bullhorn was talking again. Desperation tinged his words red and made them thin, sharp. Jaime ignored him. He was probably going on and on about wanting him to drop his gun. More cars pulled up all around him. They added sounds to the chaos. Jaime could see them out there, fidgeting behind their cars, aiming their weapons at him, adjusting their bulletproof vests, screaming nonsense. He knew they were all nervous. They were all the kind of cops who hope to make a dollar and go home unscathed every day of their career. None of them wanted to die. Not in the street, under the hot sun. Not at the hands of a man who just left prison. Not in front of people who might judge them for not neutralizing the threat immediately.

The cops reminded him of too many COs he'd met inside. Scared. Vulnerable. Hiding their fears under fake bravado. He felt sorry for them.

Jaime stood there and looked at the men behind the cars, crouching behind open doors. Each one of them was a problem, another nail in the coffin of his freedom. The pity he'd felt for them vanished. Anger filled the space it had occupied. Cookie deserved what he got. Any man would happily fuck up anyone who dared put a hand on his mother. These idiots were failing to understand that basic principle. The right thing to do would be to get back in their cars and disappear. Jaime knew they wouldn't do that. They smelled blood now. They had him trapped, and like any hunter, they wanted to finish what they'd started.

The gun in his hand felt heavy, but not impossible to lift. He brought it up.

The first shot pinged against the side of the car. Cookie's car. The idea of it getting shot made Jaime smile. He squeezed the trigger at the loudmouth with the bullhorn. The right side of his face became red mist as he spun, threw the bullhorn up, and disappeared. For a second, the white bullhorn looked like a misshaped bird trying to reach the clouds.

The explosion of gunfire sounded like a crumbling building. Something punched Jaime in the chest. His right thigh erupted in pain. His left arm was pushed back by an unseen force, the bone inside breaking with a loud crack he felt in the back of his skull. A ball of fire lit up his stomach. Pings and thuds accompanied the bullets that perforated the Impala, rocking it a bit.

The car was still moving when Jaime took a step back and placed his back against it. It was warm, welcoming.

The gun clattered to the ground, scratching against the asphalt.

Jaime looked at the red and blue lights. They swam in all directions. Tiny tendrils of light flew into the air, retracted, and flew out again.

Tiny red and blue hearts.

Tiny colorful angels.

Misplaced Christmas lights.

Chunks of neon signs reflecting in a puddle.

They were beautiful in a way Jaime couldn't quite comprehend, but he felt them tugging at his eyes, his soul, his breath.

There were too many screams. It all sounded like a single voice. It faded a bit, replaced by an army of ants that marched into his ears. His own breathing became a ragged, wet thing stuck in his throat.

A cop stepped away from his car and took a few steps forward, screaming something at Jaime with his gun held in front of his face. The gun shook. The man looked angry and scared. A vein bulged in his neck above his too-tight uniform. Spittle flew out of his mouth with each syllable.

The heat in Jaime's belly was making it hard to breathe. His leg hurt too much to stand on it. He slowly slid down the side of the car and sat on the ground. The hot asphalt penetrated his jeans and hurt him, but he didn't have the strength to stand back up.

He looked down at his pants. They were covered in blood. It shone under the sun like all wet things do. The fire in his stomach was growing sharp wings, slashing his innards to pieces as it moved around, making it impossible to think. Jaime felt his face twist into a grimace as a cough erupted from his mouth in a splash of red.

Underneath the red and blue lights, the black paint of the patrol cars was growing, invading the space occupied by white. It was rolling off the cars and melting into the asphalt. Soon it took over everything but the lights and only the red and blue angels remained, all screaming at the same time, drowning the tiny voices of the cops that were still addressing him.

Only the pain, the sound, and the lights existed.

Blood. Life liked blood. Life was like a gang: blood in, blood out. Jaime felt the precious liquid flowing out of his body, exiting it in a rush through each of the new holes the cops had given him in exchange for a righteous act. The blood knew. It was baptizing him, granting him his freedom.

He closed his eyes and thought about his mother. Her eyes. The lines around her mouth. Her smell. The rebellious hairs that refused to stay inside her bun. The ugly, frayed robe with the blue flowers she'd had since before he was born. He thought about her smacking him with a notebook when he refused to do his homework. He remembered her quietly sobbing in the kitchen while frying him some chicken. He remembered how much he'd missed her while inside.

He thought about not going back to prison now. He thought about freedom. About home. About the future.

He opened his eyes to a present that mocked his every wish and shattered any vision that dared go past it.

Then came the silence.

The red and blue angels stopped weeping. The tendrils of light came at him. They entered his eyes and flashed in his brain. They took the pain away. Jaime realized he had stopped struggling to breathe, and he asked the angels to take him with them.

ALMA

The man sitting across from Alma was like an echo of the memory of a nightmare. The leering eyes, the licking of the lips, the ill-fitting suit, the creepy tone. She'd experienced these things so many times that they all blended together in something akin to the sound of an airplane's engine. This particular man also liked to lift his left eyebrow whenever he said something he thought was funny, or whenever he asked a question. It was a cheesy, practiced move. Alma hated him from the second she'd walked into his posh, overly-decorated office. She knew what the suit was meant to convey. She understood that the huge mahogany desk should be read as "Power sits here." The insipid art and plaques on the wall were meant to communicate a perfect balance between business and an appreciation of beautiful things. Most of the art probably came from a department store or some website. Alma hated all of it because it was all a performance, and she could see right through it. The only reason she was putting up with it was the venue. A huge, free venue. The man also had contacts in a few of the city's top publications. *The Chronicle. Today. What To Do. The Statesman. The Horn.* They were all willing, he said, to run pieces on her if she could guarantee him something people would never forget.

The man, Mr. Wilson, had contacted her through her website. He was starting a new performance art series and wanted to get the buzz going. "A little entrepreneurial project," he called it. Alma had no interest in knowing how or why he had come to own an awesome old theatre near the center of downtown Austin. She also disliked the fact that he wanted half of whatever was made at the door, plus everything that was made at the bar, but Alma had no other prospects, and she knew that opportunity was allergic to knocking. She had agreed to the meeting after researching him a bit. Apparently he wasn't a psycho or a rapist. The university had a fund under his name that helped kids whose parents had been hit with medical expenses get through college. He liked to be present whenever a ribbon was cut or something was officially inaugurated. He came from money, and those who come from money mostly keep themselves in money. The man, Alma read, had worked as a high executive at a bank for a while and then made a killing by backing his son's friends when they started developing apps. There was no information anywhere on how many of them he'd invested in, but two of them took off and the man was set for life. Now he wanted to get into the arts.

"Way I see it, you get to do what you do best with a bit of an advertising machine behind you, and we both make money because of it. You don't pay a cent and I don't have to invest in anything except the liquor, and if I know one thing, it's that there's never a problem selling booze. Plus, my buddy Mike downtown already helped me…expedite the process of acquiring permits, so everything is already good to go. Sound good to you?"

Alma nodded. A free venue. Free publicity. Mr. Wilson was probably going to try to sleep with her, but that was something she already knew. It was something a man like him would try even if he offered nothing in return. Entitlement poured out of each pore in his body. To money. To her. To respect. To everything. Entitlement. White privilege. Rich blood. Connections. It all added up to a life she couldn't imagine. It all added up to a life that was contrary to everything she knew. It all added up to something she wanted to destroy. However, she agreed with him. She wanted this. Besides the creepiness and eerily perfect timing, the proposal seemed legit. In fact, if everything was as great as he said, she was even willing to let him think there was a chance of something going down between them. A dog will never run as fast as it does when there's something it wants running in front of it.

She knew he was waiting for some verbal response, but the images in her head kept her quiet. She stared into the man's sharp blue eyes, which would have been gorgeous in the face of a gentler, purer creature, and thought about grabbing a pen from his desk and gouging them out. The visions were plenty. They came at her all times of day now. Dead people. Body parts. Puddles of blood. Chunks of flesh teeming with maggots. Discarded bones. Screams in the middle of the night. At first it was too much. It was scary and unwelcome. Then she understood that she had plugged into something ethereal, something supernatural. Most artists waited their whole lives to get in touch with something like that and get inspired by it. She wasn't even thirty yet and it was happening. She had accepted it, and immediately started feeling the need for the real thing. She was angry and frustrated, and something was telling her that making assholes bleed was the only way to improve her mood. She had always been familiar with her righteous anger and her inability to put up with bullshit, but lately her feelings had changed. She no longer wanted to destroy the patriarchy through discourse. She no longer enjoyed the thought of eviscerating some young dumbass who cat-called her on the sidewalk. No, her thoughts had shifted and now she wanted to eviscerate them in the physical sense of the word. She wanted to gut idiots like fish for real. She wanted to run a serrated knife across their flabby pale guts so she could see their intestines unspool and drop to the floor with a wet plop as they struggled to accept that they were touchable, fallible, destructible, soft.

"Well, if everything sounds good to you, we're good to get the ball rolling on this thing. I already have Stephan McMichael performing this week. Friday night, I think. He can't do Saturday because he has a thing in New Orleans he has to drive to. Anyway, he's some guy who swallows all kinds of things and then brings them back up. Kinda like a magician, but he uses his stomach most of the time. He's covered in tattoos and performs in nothing but a loincloth. Haha. Women love him. You think you can do Saturday? Can you have something ready to go by then? Something good?"

Saturday. That gave her a couple of days. She didn't need much time. All she had to purchase was easily available, and she was ready to improvise her intro. Plus, she had been reading a lot about the Orishas since her last piece, which she realized while editing touched on many interesting things about her Caribbean identity.

"Don't worry, Mr. Wilson, I've been working on what I consider my best piece yet. I assure you people will be talking about it for months."

"Hell yeah, they will! That's the kind of attitude I like," he said.

He leaned over his desk and stretched out his hand. She shook it. When she tried to pull way, Mr. Wilson held on to it, looking at her and smiling. A bullshit power move. It sickened her. She used her left hand to slap the desk. Hard. The photos on the desk rattled. Mr. Wilson let go of her hand and jumped back. The underside of his chair screamed in agony. She winked at him and stood up.

"I'm looking forward to Saturday, Mr. Wilson. Any way I could check out the theatre before then? I want to have a better idea of the space I'll be working with."

"Uh…yeah, sure," he said.

Mr. Wilson looked down, opened a drawer in his desk, and pulled out a key attached to a small keychain of a chubby unicorn.

"I have three or four copies. All you artists want to know what you're working with. Haha."

She took the key and thanked him. Despite the awful man in front of her, Alma couldn't keep herself from smiling.

LA BRUJA

Inmaculada stood where the truck had been and felt her soul crack in half. Her invisible body produced no tears, but she felt sadness pour out of her and pool in the indentations the trailer's wheels had left in the dirt. In the waning light, it looked like shadows cast by strange flying creatures that moved too slowly to remain airborne. Much like oil from an old car or the blood of slaughtered animals, her sadness would stain the ground. Her shadow tears would become temporary marks that would eventually be washed away by rain and wind, much like everything is obliterated by the way the world keeps on keeping on regardless of our tragedies. Inmaculada knew all this, but she didn't care. The real scars were in the hearts and souls of those who'd lost loved ones inside that damn trailer. Those were the scars she was avenging. That was the pain she was redressing. Those were the deaths whose echo she inhabited for the time being.

With pain throbbing throughout her new form, Inmaculada circled the space where the trailer had been, soothing the earth underneath it and pushing hungry spirits away from the souls that still lingered, confused and scared.

The truck had been there for three days before the authorities had shown up. Someone reported the presence of the vehicle and probably guessed what it contained. With crumpled faces they had shown up and opened the back of the trailer to expose the nightmare within. Bloated bodies. Swarms of flies. The many liquids contained in the human body pushed out by decay. The heat and the smell had flown out of it like an invisible hammer.

The scene had been too much for some. A few men vomited, careful to move away from others and bending over to protect their black shoes. Other crossed themselves, sent up prayers to Dios and Jesús and La Virgen and todos los santos as they wondered out loud how Dios could keep letting things like this happen. Others shook their head and allowed their solemn silence to speak for them. Inmaculada felt the anger emanating from some of them, a blistering, powerful thing that heated the air around them and pushed their blood closer to the surface. From others, she only received sorrow or indifference. She knew those unaffected had probably already seen too much. You can only witness so much of the world's ugliness before your soul becomes a dull, damaged, hardened thing.

The men made phone calls and used the equipment in their cars to report the finding. Then came the white vans. Men and women wearing masks and latex gloves packed the bodies into black bags, zipped them up, and loaded them into the backs of the vans. The process was quiet, ceremonial. Every time they pulled a kid out, everyone looked down, refusing to make eye contact with the others. They were temporarily ashamed of being human.

Seeing those people handle the bodies stirred the maelstrom of feelings inside Inmaculada until it threatened to become a black hole that would swallow the world. Watching them stash the bloated, dripping bodies away ripped away the last remaining shred of humanity held in her eyes and electrified the sense of loss that flowed through her like blood. Those people, those mothers and fathers and sisters and brothers and sons and daughters and cousins and friends and lovers were now putrefying meat, a problem that had to be taken care of before the smell got any worse. Her husband was a rotting thing, a dribbling sack of festering meat. No laughter came from his mouth. No fingers came up to caress his mustache when he was concentrating. His strong, tanned arms would no longer hold her son as his lips blew raspberries on his stomach, making the child laugh in a way that injected light into the walls of every room in the house. No snoring would ever again escape his throat and make her think of a wounded bird. The smell of earth and cologne would never jump out at her from his neck as he walked by. His small, shiny eyes would never look out the window again as he sipped his coffee and planned a better future for them.

Her husband as she had known him and loved him was gone.

Erased.

Annihilated.

Defeated.

Conquered by death.

While she fully understood a reunion was coming, she also felt a longing for the immediate beauty and pleasure the physical world afforded them. She craved it. She missed it. The finality of death was partial, but the part it took away was so close to her still, so fresh in her memory, that its importance overpowered all promises of a reunion.

The thing in the black bag was a nothing but a corpse. She ached to see his spirit now, but her work was not yet done.

Eventually a skinny man with a tiny golden cross ear-ring in his left ear and a tattoo of a rose on his right hand and a tall woman with haunted eyes and very short nails pulled Inmaculada's son out of the trailer and placed him on top of a bag. His tongue was swollen, forcing his mouth open. His eyes were closed. He looked like an overstuffed plastic version of her son instead of the real thing. His smell was gone. His laughter would never reach her ears again. His tears would never soak her shoulder. His tiny body was done twisting and turning in bed at night, done running to hug her legs with the impetus that only inhabits children, done playing and jumping and experiencing new things.

She remembered carrying him inside, showing him the songs her mother had shown her. She remembered the pain of giving birth. She remembered the sleepless nights. She remembered his first two teeth, impossibly painful on her nipples. She remembered his smart questions, his bizarre observations, the face he made as a baby whenever he saw a bird take to the sky and the joy in his face whenever they saw a dog. She remembered his endless energy. But above all that she remembered the love. It was impossible to describe, impossible to explain, impossible to measure. After the loss of her first son to violence, her second baby had been salvation. The reason for everything. The center of her universe.

The pain inside her ballooned, reached its breaking point, and exploded. She screamed. Everyone around the trailer stopped in their tracks. They looked around.

"Qué demonios fué eso, Martita?" asked the skinny man who was handling Inmaculada's son.

The woman shook her head and looked around once more, her eyes passing over Inmaculada but not seeing her. The woman had children of her own. Inmaculada knew it because she was at once her and many people, her blood twice sacred by having fed a new life. It was written in her aura. She understood the scream in a way she couldn't share.

"Date prisa, Martín. No quiero estar aquí más tiempo del que sea necesario," she replied, letting the man's question hang in the air, unanswered but as present as the trailer itself.

Inmaculada couldn't keep watching. She sank back into the earth, letting the warm soil shoot the energy of the small shrubs and crawling insects all around her, into her new body. She focused on that, feeding on the energy to stay on this side of the veil.

That night she would chant longer than ever. Everything she carried and felt and longed for would go into her words. They had taken love from her, and she was going to give them hate in return. A hate they hadn't seen before. A

135

hate that would destroy anything it encountered. A hate so deep and passionate it could only come from the devastated corpse of the most profound, all-encompassing, unconditional love ever felt. She was going to give them the kind of hate only a mother could feel.

PEDRITO

For years Pedrito had heard stories about the creatures that lived in the desert and came out to hunt at night. He'd heard all about La Llorona. She had drowned her children in the river out of spite, and regret had kept her glued to this earth, roaming the desert at night and crying, hunting for children to take with her to the river to do the same thing. His abuelo had also told him about El Cucuy. He walked the streets at night, hiding in alleyways and under windows, looking for children who were misbehaving. He had big teeth and eyes that never closed. Depending on who told you the story, he also carried around a burlap sack to stuff children in before disappearing back into the night. For years, every shadow that passed near his window at night had been El Cucuy. Then there was El Cadejo, a giant ghost dog who enjoyed feasting on the flesh of children who dared stay away from home at night. Lastly, there was El Chupacabra. This one he had learned about in school, and it freaked him out more than the rest. As he had grown, the mythical beasts and monsters his abuelo had spoken about retreated from his mind. They belonged to his early years, were part of his childhood. Now that he was able to read, he knew they were part of his culture, part of the folklore of many South American and Caribbean countries, all of which put their own spin on the tales, but none of them were real. They were stories you told children to make them behave. The Chupacabra was different. It mutilated goats and other animals. There were no photos of La Llorona online, but there were plenty of photos of drained, mutilated cattle, and Pedrito had seen most of them. He was sure the creature was out there now, prowling the desert in search of warm blood. Every sound he heard could be coming from it. Every strange shadow could be its shape. Every second he spent with his eyes closed was one more second the monster or alien or whatever it was could use to get closer to him.

"Si quieres descansar un poco, descansa ahora," said Santos.

He was sitting across from Pedrito, dragging a dirty spoon along the bottom of a can of spaghetti he'd opened with a knife and slurped cold.

"I'm not tired," Pedrito replied.

Santos chuckled.

Over the past two days, Pedrito had observed Santos. The man seemed to always be in a good mood, even when he was serious. Strange things made him smile or chuckle. Sometimes he would shake his head and laugh as if remembering an old joke. He didn't speak much. Other times, he sat there and stared at nothing, unmoving, until he snapped out of it the way some people snap out of a nightmare.

After Pedrito shot the man from the roof, it'd taken Santos a couple of minutes to stop laughing. After he stopped, he had dragged the corpse and dropped it next to the other two bodies in the tiny, smelly room. Then he had taken the rifle away from the man and removed his shoes. "These we're gonna leave in the desert, at one of the spots where people leave water for those making the trip," he'd said. "Many people need shoes when crossing the border, y este pinche huevón is not gonna need them any more. You have to care about the living, kid, because the dead don't matter, unless you believe in ghosts."

Another thing Santos did was switch between English and Spanish more than anyone Pedrito had ever spoken with, including his own father. He also used words that belonged to neither language, words he had taken from

English and bent into Spanish. For example, he said tro-
ka for truck and told him they were going to wachar the
milicianos instead of watch them. It reminded Pedrito of
his father, the way he tried to speak as much English as
possible, because he was convinced speaking the language
fluidly would open doors for all of them once they had
enough money to pay the coyote.

Santos leaned back and stared at Pedrito.

"You don't wanna sleep because you're hungry. Quieres sangre. Si te despistas, sales del desierto convertido en
hombre lobo…bueno, algo así."

A werewolf. He had no idea why Santos was bringing
them up now. He didn't care. He knew that, if he allowed
him to talk, he'd eventually get around to telling him what
they were going to do a bit later.

"Hay dos maneras de ser asesino en esta vida, carnalito.
Some people become killers porque la vida les hace algo.
They want revenge. They kill one or two or a hundred people to right a wrong, entiendes? The other kind of people…
well, those are born, nacen. There is something inside them
that makes them kill. They do it time and again. They never get tired. They always want more. It's as if death has
blessed them in a special way, de manera tal que se alimen-
tan or agarran fuerza de aquellos que matan. Yo sé que un

miliciano mató a tu papa y que estás lleno de odio, que quieres venganza. I can see that. Vengeance is something that's hard to hide. It makes your skin hot and your eyes shiny. It's kinda like a fever. Anybody who knows how to look can see that. So, yeah, you want blood for your daddy's blood. Eso es justo. I understand that. Pero tu eres de los otros. You will kill any miliciano, not just the one who killed your papá. You want them all dead. You are not a revenge killer. Tu eres un lobo, carnalito. You were born to kill. You have the voice inside you. You want to please la Huesuda, to keep her well-fed. You're like me. You don't give a fuck. Haha! That's good. La frontera es un sitio malo, especially if you start caring about shit. La frontera es un sitio donde hay que ser un hijo de puta para sobrevivir. You have that, mijo. Don't lose it. Nunca."

Pedrito listened to the words Santos was saying to him and realized the man was right. The man who had killed his father was dead. He had seen his head blast open and his blood hit the ground, but that wasn't enough. The empty space inside him was infinite. The raging hatred in his chest was a fire no amount of death would be able to put out. He had no idea when all of it had started, but he understood there were things about death, pain, loss, and anger that kids his age weren't ready to understand. He was fine

141

with that. He wanted to kill milicianos. He wanted to kill members of la migra. That was enough for him. The thing inside him was pushing him forward, making him certain that what he was doing was the right thing. There would be blood, and if that made him a werewolf, then he'd scream at the moon and dare the fucking Chupacabra to try to come and get him.

THE MOTHER

The sun was out in full force. Its rays hit the tiny bathroom window at 186,000 miles per hour and shattered against the glass without breaking it. She'd learned the speed from one of The Boy's most recent science projects for school. The number stuck with her for some reason. Now she focused on it. It was inconceivable to her. So was the fact that light just splintered into sustained rays of blinding whiteness that hung in the air near the window like a cluster of solid spikes instead of blasting her into oblivion.

The Mother pulled her eyes away from the light and looked back at her face in the mirror above the bathroom sink. Whatever was going on in her mouth was something she had no desire to deal with. There was a dull pain that made her think of cavities, but too many teeth were moving around in there.

The first one had been a molar on the upper left side of her jaw. She felt it move around while trying to eat with The Boy a couple of nights before. She'd spent the next few hours mindlessly pushing her tongue against it, feeling it move. It reminded her of being a girl and losing her teeth, her father coming up with a slew of bizarre ways of yanking them out once it was time to do so. This, however, felt different. It was wrong. She took good care of her teeth. They looked healthy. Now they didn't feel that way. She'd only stopped fidgeting with it later that night, when the movement started. Her body had become stiff, almost immovable. The idea that the monster in her uterus was controlling her scared her so much that she welcomed the immobility. Tears of fear, anger, and frustration rolled down the side of her face as the creature exited her and vanished into the night like it always did. She waited for its return in silence, trying to keep her mind away from the beast, trying not to imagine it feeding on a baby in town.

She passed out from exhaustion long before the creature returned. She was thankful to just feel it slide back into its space without having to see the scant moonlight reflected on its slick, blood-covered body. She was thankful she hadn't had to look once again at those tiny, hideous human hands.

Now The Mother opened her mouth and stared at the mess inside. Blood and saliva had turned parts of her gums a shiny, darker shade of pink than the rest of her mouth. She grabbed the molar that had been moving the most and tried it. It moved all the way to the left and remained attached to her only by a thin portion of gum. She pulled. The tooth came out with an almost inaudible snap. Her mouth filled with the coppery taste of blood.

Gurgling saltwater was supposed to help, but it only made her gums sting and she felt it flow under a few other teeth. She spat the pink, foamy water out and opened her mouth again.

The second molar she grabbed with her stiff fingers came off even faster than the first one. She stared at the two holes in her mouth. Her tongue moved to them instinctively, exploring the strange new space the way a dog would sniff all the corners of a new house. A fleeting thought crossed her mind. She pictured a dentist looking into her ruined mouth and shaking his head. Her doctor would ask questions, make recommendations, and schedule her for more appointments so he could take a bunch of measurements and eventually give her some prosthetics. She had no time for that. Money was an issue. Much like her grandmother, she would reach old age with a graveyard for a mouth; a desolate place punctuated by a few dark protrusions marking the space where something good and healthy once stood.

Standing in front of the mirror, with her tongue darting and blood dripping from her lips, The Mother felt the humanity ebbing out of her. She was becoming the human version of the hard case cicadas leave behind. She was becoming a solid egg for the thing inside her, and it would crack her forever when it finally decided to come out for good. She was becoming a chrysalis, and chrysalises eventually become leftover, discarded things, dead remnants, abandoned homes.

By the time The Boy returned from school, there were nine teeth piled in a semicircle around the sink's drain. Thick bloody saliva had pooled on top and around them, coating them in a thin layer of pinkish tackiness that grabbed the light and made it look like the teeth were moving. She kept spitting, not wanting to swallow the blood, which was, according to a voice in her head, cursed. The viscous mix had dripped down her chin and stained her beige shirt. Hearing the door slam brought her back to the present. There was no time to clean everything, so she focused on throwing the teeth in the toilet and flushing, running some water on the sink, and stuffing her shirt in the hamper before pulling out a dirty white shirt from the top and throwing it over her head.

When she stepped out, The Boy was in the kitchen, a glass of water in hand, drinking in that animalistic way children drink when the sun and the heat have pulled too much moisture from their system. He looked at her.

"¿Mamá? ¿Estás bien?"

At that moment, the question was too large to answer. It flew out of The Boy's mouth and impaled her with a thousand invisible knives. The answer was no. The answer was crying, falling down in despair. The answer was walking up to The Boy and showing him the gory disaster zone inside her mouth. The answer was pushing past The Boy, opening the kitchen drawer to his left, pulling out a knife, and slicing her own throat to make the madness stop.

No.

The Boy.

She wouldn't do any of that.

The only conceivable answer was a lie. The only possible answer was a yes. The only feasible answer was a short, positive reply that contained a multiplicity of promises at its core. The only answer was a yes that bridged the gap between the disgusting plink each tooth made as it dropped on the sink's porcelain and whatever wet noise the creature inside her would make when she sliced it to pieces and burned those abominable chunks.

Keeping her lips closed, The Mother smiled. The love in her chest warmed her, sent blood out to her extremities, gave her the strength to move toward The Boy despite the fact that every step took as much effort as pushing a car uphill.

She walked past The Boy and kissed the top of his head, stopping briefly to inhale the miraculous smell of dirt, sweat, and his own unique aroma.

"¿Tienes hambre?"

"Mucha. ¿Qué hay de comer?"

"Por ahora nada," she said, her heart breaking a bit more under the weight of an unexpected bout of guilt. "Sal a jugar media hora y horita preparo algo."

The Boy said yes. His smile lifted the corners of his mouth and pressed his cheeks closer to his shiny black eyes. The Mother drank it in.

The door slammed again. The Mother reached up to her neck. Her skin was dry. It felt like touching the scales of a dry fish. Her fingers had lost most of their mobility, but they still obeyed her somewhat. She grabbed the old rosary around her neck and pulled it out. The same light that had been coming into the bathroom bathed the kitchen with its high-speed warmth. The Mother turned to it, rosary clasped like a small, miraculous solution to the nightmare that engulfed her, and she prayed.

"Dios te salve, Reina y Madre de misericordia, vida, dulzura y esperanza nuestra. Dios te salve. A ti llamamos los desterrados hijos de Eva; a ti suspiramos, gimiendo y llorando, en este valle de lágrimas. Ea, pues, Señora, aboga- da nuestra, vuelve a nosotros esos tus ojos misericordiosos, y después de este destierro muéstranos a Jesús, fruto ben- dito de tu vientre. Oh clementísima, oh piadosa, oh dulce siempre Virgen María."

She squeezed the rosary so hard with her numb hand that she didn't notice the blood dripping from her closed fist until after she finished praying.

THE COYOTE

Clemencia was the person the coyote went to see when he needed orders. Padre Frank was the person he went to see when he needed guidance.

Padre Frank lived just outside of town in a small shack behind his church. He was a tall, skinny man who never stepped outside his shack without his cassock, even in the middle of summer. The coyote had met him ten years before, when the man had first shown up and taken over for Padre Sebastián after he mysteriously disappeared. Padre Frank was strange and unlike any other padre the coyote had ever met, but a bizarre encounter had made them friends.

The coyote drove out to Padre Frank's place with the radio off, allowing his thoughts about his dream about La Virgencita to take over. He wanted to ask Padre Frank about it, so having it fresh in his memory would be a good thing.

He parked next to a dying shrub about ten feet from the shack's door, parked, killed the motor, and stared at the dilapidate place with its dirty, peeling off-white walls and corrugated zinc roof. It looked more like a tiny crackhouse than the home of a man of the cloth.

A yellowish light came from the only window in the front of the place. That meant Padre Frank was in. The coyote left the car, walked up to the door, and rapped his knuckles against it. A few seconds of silence followed. The coyote could hear a bit of rustling going on behind the door. A chair scraped against the floor. Then came Padre Frank's raspy voice.

"¿Quién llama?"

Padre Frank was a gringo, and his accent made it clear. Instead of having the accent on the *e*, he placed it on the *i*. Also, he couldn't pronounce *llama*, so the whole thing came out as *¿Quíen yiama?*

"Abre la puerta, pinche gringo, que un cura siempre debe estar dispuesto a atender a sus feligreses," he replied with a smile on his face.

There was another half minute of silence and then the dilapidated wooden door creaked open. Padre Frank stood in the doorway in full regalia even though it was close to

151

midnight and still too warm to wear anything but shorts and a t-shirt.

"The child savior is here," said Padre Frank. "Come in so I can take this fucking thing off."

The coyote stepped into the shack and closed the door behind him. Padre Frank made his way to a small table, lifted the cassock over his head, folded it over his arm, and placed it on the back of one of the two chairs.

The coyote looked at his tattoo-covered body and, even though he had seen the ink many times before, had a hard time not saying something or pulling out his piece and putting a bullet between the man's eyes.

Right below Padre Frank's neck was a gigantic black and grey eagle with its head to the side. The tips of its wings reached Padre Frank's shoulders. In the bird's talons was a black shield with SS twin bolts in the middle. Underneath that, a fading swastika could still be seen next to a woman holding a rifle and a screaming skull surrounded by flames. Just above the waist of the man's blue shorts were two words in a blocky font: WHITE PRIDE. The rest of his torso was a hodgepodge of numbers, snakes, faces, cards, indistinguishable words and numbers, and skulls. Most of it was prison ink, so it sported the bluish, perennially fading hue of guitar string and shitty radio motor machine that prison tattoos share.

Padre Frank's arms were a continuation of the themes that covered his torso. SS bolts. Guns. Naked women. Swastikas. A musclebound man with a large gun holding a Confederate flag. SWP across his left forearm. AB and a celtic cross on the inside of his right forearm. The coyote knew there was also a portrait of Hitler on his right thigh. Padre Frank had shown it to him on one of their drunken nights together after a job. White and pink scar lines crisscrossed Hitler's face from when Padre Frank had tried to slash the ink to make it unrecognizable.

Padre Frank grabbed a bottle from the table, plucked a lit cigarette from the plate serving as his ashtray and sat on the same chair he'd used to hang his cassock.

"What brings you here this late, desert man?"

The coyote walked up to the table, pulled out the second chair, and sat across from Padre Frank.

"There's bad things happening at la frontera, Padrecito. La jefa said I need to stay low and not do shit until she tells me it's okay to go back, but I feel useless if I'm not doing God's work. You know how it is."

"I know what you're talking about, man. I've been reading the news. There's the political bad stuff and the bad stuff that is not directly tied to the hands of men, you hear what I'm saying? Right now both evils are at their peak for reasons I can't begin to comprehend. A couple nights ago I had to put two men under the dirt. Selena gave me a call. One of them had a hookup in ICE. They're disappearing children, selling them to whoever pays the most. It makes me sick. These fuckers I'm telling you about were bringing back two girls. Four and six years old, if you can fucking believe it. Not even teenagers, man. A fucking shame. Selena knew where the trade was gonna happen, so I had to show up before they did. Brought the Big Mac with me and set up in a nearby hill. Thankfully the fucking sumbitches showed up early and I took them out with minimal fuzz. Driver didn't even have time to step outta the truck before I blew his head off. The girls were in the back, sweating like whores in church under a false seat. Selena came by here after and picked them up. You could say it was a routine gig, but it didn't feel that way. God is merciful and I thanked Him for allowing me to spill the blood of bad men without suffering injury myself, but something about the area just felt off, kinda like when you walk into a room and the people there were having a bad fight right until the second you walked in."

First, Clemencia had spoken around the issue. Now, Padre Frank was doing the same. It made the coyote feel frustrated. He just wanted to carry on doing his work and

154

helping any way he could. He knew that appealing to Padre Frank's love for kids was the way to go. After all, after fifteen years in prison, a few of them as a killer for the Aryan Brotherhood, the man had talked to God in a dream. That's how he had ended up as a priest in a small frontera town.

"Pero Padre Frank, la frontera siempre ha sido un lugar feo. I get that you and la jefecita are worried about something, but unless there's a specific reason not to, I don't understand why I have to sit at home with my arms crossed while there are kids waiting to cross."

"Is that why you're here? Boss lady done told you not to go and you want my blessing to go against what she said? You're crazy, man. I wouldn't cross that woman." Padre Frank took a swig of the bottle he was holding and shook his head.

The coyote looked at him. His thin, pale, ink-covered skin spoke of years of hard living. How many men had he killed? How many times would he risk it all to save children in order to make up for half a life of wrong actions and awful ideas?

"Nah, I don't want that. I came to see you because I've been having a dream. A holy dream. Veo a La Virgencita. Ella me dice que debo ir, que algo malo está pasando y yo tengo que ayudarle a ponerle fin al asunto. In my dream, she shows up riding a…ball of light and then kills two men who are torturing two kids."

Padre Frank kept his head down. The cigarette was now more ash than anything. The ash curved down, but Padre Frank's immobility prevented it from falling. He finally spoke, his voice calm but sounding like was speaking more to himself than to the coyote.

"The motherfuckers bringing the kids back are definitely something we need to take care of soon. We need to send them a message. Even if that fucking orange buffoon insists on putting kids in cages, kids being trafficked is not something we're gonna put up with. Maybe that's why the Virgin is calling you to the border. I guess I could tell you where the traffickers, militia assholes, and ICE contacts meet so you can…"

The coyote sat up and pulled out his gun. Padre Frank dropped the cigarette and his hand was suddenly in front of him, holding a .45. The gun was steady despite the speed with which he'd pulled it out. The coyote smiled.

"For a man in direct contact with God you put a lot of trust on that gun of yours, Padrecito. Relax. I only want to give you this thing so you can bless it for me."

Padre Frank smiled, but didn't lower the gun. The coyote looked into his eyes and saw something deadly in them.

That made him remember the night he'd found out the priest was not a priest. He had been hearing stories about an old man, a shoemaker who made shoes for rich ladies, having a taste for prepubescent girls. He stalked him for a while. After a week, he watched the man open his garage door to a strange white car. The coyote knew what was up. He broke in through the kitchen. He found the shoemaker and the man who'd brought him the girl dead, large bullet holes dripping blood and brains on the beige carpet. A few feet from them stood Padre Frank, with the same .45 he was holding now in his hand. They had a short conversation and quickly came to the conclusion that they should work together from time to time to keep kids safe and the streets a little cleaner.

"Yeah, I can do that," said Padre Frank. "Better to send you into battle with some backup than all by your lonesome. Slide that thing over to me slowly and I'll sprinkle some holy water on it, my man."

Padre Frank finally lowered his gun, but he didn't put it away. The coyote looked at him sitting there as he slid the gun in his direction, pushing it by the barrel to keep the religious ex-con at ease. He tried to imagine for the umpteenth time what his life would be like if he had to hide most of his skin from people at all times. He wondered what he would do if people saw his naked arms and immediately judged him and hated him. Then, for the first time, he realized that the questions he had asked himself so many times were stupid. He was a brown man, and for many people, the color of his skin was as bad as the images on Padre Frank's body.

When the gun was close enough, the coyote pulled his hand back across the table. His eyes were locked on Padre Frank's. Both men came from darkness and dealt with it regularly. This made them distrustful. Yes, they were friendly acquaintances and hated the same kind of people, but they were also lone wolves with a knack for violence. They could kill each other without blinking if the time came where such a thing was needed. The coyote knew they both existed in a place outside of normal social contracts and standard social behavior. He was fine with that, and he reminded himself that the man now grabbing his gun had killed many men simply because they belonged to a different race or an enemy gang.

Padre Frank killed his cigarette on the plate in front of him and took one more swig on the brown bottle he was holding before placing it on the table. He then took the gun, lifted it, and aimed it at the wall.

"Hell of a piece you got here, desert man," he said.

Then he stood up and walked to the night table next to his bed. He opened the drawer and pulled out a small white plastic bottle.

"This…Virgencita you got here, you sure she's calling to you, man?"

For a second the coyote was angry. Was Padre Frank, who wasn't even a real fucking priest, doubting his dream? Then he realized the man was only forcing him to realize what he was about to do.

"Yeah, Padre, I am sure she was speaking to me."

Frank nodded. He walked back to the table and placed the gun on it. Then he unscrewed the cap and splashed a bit of holy water on the grip.

"Remember Deuteronomy 20:1, desert man: *When you go out to battle against your enemies and see horses and chariots and people more numerous than you, do not be afraid of them; for the LORD your God, who brought you up from the land of Egypt, is with you.*"

Frank turned the gun over and repeated the process. With each movement of his skinny arms, the muscles in his chest twitched. The eagle shook. Then he lifted the gun by the barrel and offered it to the coyote.

"Ecclesiastes 3:8 tells us there is a time to love, and a time to hate; a time for war, and a time for peace. The time for war is here. The time to save souls is here. The devil walks the desert. Evil corrupts the souls of children in the name of a law that is of man and not of heaven. Trump is the devil. ICE is the devil. The gangs that push good people to leave the safety of their home are the devil. Traffickers are the devil. Child molesters are the devil. You are the Lord's sword. I am the Lord's sword. We are the Lord's avengers."

The coyote grabbed the gun. Electricity ran down his arm. His chest filled with something akin to joy. It was the realization that he was a holy warrior, a chosen man who'd do God's work.

"I will tell you where to go. If the Virgin wants you to go there, I have no doubts you will return in one piece. Pull that trigger righteously. Remember Ezekiel 7:25 if doubts assail you: *I will execute great vengeance on them with wrathful rebukes. Then they will know that I am the Lord, when I lay my vengeance upon them.*"

The coyote nodded, cradling his gun near his chest with both hands.

"Now listen up. The wicked den isn't far from here, especially if you know the border."

ALMA

The audience was buzzing. Their sound reached Alma's ears and tickled her in ways she'd never been tickled before. She was excited and nervous and eager to start.

Underneath her clothes, the bags of pigs' blood were warm. The skin underneath them was wet. Sweat ran down her body, cooling as it moved.

The machete in her hands had a sticker at the base. The one hanging from her hip did not. They were very different. The one she was holding looked like a regular machete. It had been made in Ecuador. She thought one made in South America would be fitting. She bought it online because no retailers carried it in the US. It was hefty and looked as shiny as anything else she'd ever bought. The thing was two feet long. She imagined farmers in the Andes using it to keep nature at bay and to put food on the table.

She'd also read it was the machete issued to the Ecuadorian Special Forces, and that made her smile because she had started to think of herself as a special force of nature.

The machete dangling from her hip was different. It looked more like an exotic sword from a science fiction movie than a machete. It was entirely black, and heavier than the one she was holding. The top of it was blocky instead of round and much wider than the base, which made it feel more like an axe than a machete. It was only 21.5 inches long, but something about the way it looked and the fact that it was 1055 high carbon steel, which was something she'd had to research, had pushed her to buy it. It was far more expensive than she ever thought a machete could be, but special events required special sacrifices.

Thinking about the variety of machetes she had found online had forced her to think about the depth of things she'd never thought about. People create entire subcultures, entire scenes, around bizarre objects and practices the rest of humanity doesn't pay attention to. Toys, stamps, old electronics, coins, drinking tea, machetes, koi fish, books, movie posters, fancy shoes, smoking weed, baseball cards, old photographs, glassblowing, postcards, clown figurines; you can find a scene, a group, a fanbase for whatever you're into. It was a strange thought, at once comforting and scary. It bloomed in her brain, surrounded by things like *Star Wars* toys and people who enjoy collecting really hot peppers, but her mind quickly wandered away from those items and people and landed on groups that shared different sets of passions and collected different things. Nazis. Rapists. Serial killers. Pedophiles. The entitled fucks who had represented obstacles throughout her life and now sat outside waiting for her…

Outside, the buzz died down a bit. She pictured Mr. Wilson walking out and lifting his hands toward the crowd like an overweight messiah in a tailored suit. She couldn't care less about how he introduced her. He'd asked for a short bio and she'd emailed him one, but she was sure the man would try to improvise something and make a joke or two while introducing her. It didn't matter. Her actions would leave a mark and speak louder than any bio ever could.

The place was relatively small but the sound coming from outside told Alma it was fuller than she'd expected. Mr. Wilson had done his part. A few publications had paid attention, mostly because there was something new and exciting about the revamped space she was using. She didn't care. More people meant a better performance.

Alma thought about the two men outside. She felt bad about promising them another $500 after the show was over, because she knew she wasn't going to pay them, but the $500 each of them had already pocketed was more than enough to make them smile and nod enthusiastically at everything she said. Their gig was easy: barricade the front and back doors using two bizarre contraptions she'd acquired online. Once the apparatuses where in place, the men could disappear. She hoped they would be smart enough to get lost quickly.

The audience erupted in applause. It was her time to come out. She took one last look at the machete in her hand, the light running down its sharp edge like a liquid, and stood up.

The walk to the stage was short. Three steps lead up to it from the backstage area. She jumped them in a single bound and walked out with her arms raised, her head tilted to the ceiling. She knew the stage lights would catch the blade of the machete and make people immediately take notice of it.

The applause died quickly. These people knew performances like hers required silence. Alma stood there, lowered her head, and looked out at the sea of faces. She inhaled deeply before speaking.

"Suffering. Anger."

As she finished saying the second word, she used the machete to slash the sack of pig blood taped to her right thigh. She'd worn old jeans and a loose, white long-sleeved shirt to make the cutting easier and ensure the blood would be seen even from the back of the theater.

"Anger. Whitewashing. Racism."

She lifted her left arm and slashed the bag taped underneath it.

"Gaslighting. Abuse. Harassment. Rape."

The blade sliced across the big sack on her stomach. Dark blood cascaded down her front and soaked her white shirt and jeans. A few people in the audience gasped.

"Inequality. Injustice. Patriarchy."

She stopped, lowered the machete, inhaled deeply again. The warm blood was bathing her, running down her body and dripping onto the wooden floor. This was a baptism she wanted to perform for Ogún, a deity she had heard about from her grandmother a long time ago and had been obsessing about for the last couple of days for reasons she couldn't discern.

"For many of you, these are just words. For many of you, these are just things snowflakes say. For many of you, those using these words, the people feeling these things, are just supporters of dumb PC culture. For many of you, these

165

things mean nothing. If you are not a woman, women's issues are outside your realm of interest. If you are not homosexual, the struggles of homosexuals are nonissues to you. If you are not a person of color, identity politics are something we need to get rid of."

Alma stopped talking and looked out at the spectators beyond the edge of the stage. They were all paying attention.

"Now I need three volunteers. You won't have to do a thing. All I need you to do is stand here and listen to me while facing the audience."

A murmur went through the crowd, which Alma couldn't see well because of the overhead lights that stabbed her eyes.

She saw a few hands go up.

"You three in the first row, come on up."

There was movement. Bodies shuffled in front of the stage as people got up and moved toward her. Soon the sound of feet on the side stairs told Alma she would be joined by her volunteers.

The first one up was a young woman wearing a blue shirt and a long black skirt. Her sandals poked out from beneath the skirt with each step. Something shiny in them caught the light and sparkled for a second before being swallowed by the dark material again. Alma thought about the impermanence of things and smiled at the approaching woman. The young woman's hair was brown and long. It was parted down the middle and draped over her shoulders casually. The brown mane moved slightly as she walked, like heavy curtains in a slight breeze. She was thin and relatively attractive thanks to almond eyes and a clear complexion. Her blue shirt danced on her skinny torso. She had worked really hard at applying makeup in a way that would make her look like she wasn't wearing any. Alma picked her arms for her performance. In her head, this woman was already second, even though she hadn't seen the other two individuals.

The second person to climb onto the stage was a large white man with a yellow button-down shirt and khakis. He wore loafers and his hair was shot with grey and pushed to the left with some kind of gel or mousse. His ruddy cheeks spoke of a recent shave. The red nose and cheeks whispered something about high blood pressure and a stressful job. He had blue eyes under bushy eyebrows and looked like he would one day make a great grandfather. He also looked like every CEO and director and supervisor and tenured professor and business owner and racist uncle and catcalling asshole Alma had ever seen. She looked at the space between his head and round, droopy shoulders and picked that spot for her performance. She also decided he would go first. A whole life hearing "ladies first" was more than enough.

The last person was another man. He was much younger than his predecessor. He had a trimmed beard, thick black eyeglasses, and a rowdy mop of curls sitting on top of his head. He was the tallest person on the stage by at least half a foot. His curved back told Alma he was aware of his height and didn't like it when people pointed it out to him. He was thin, but not as thin as the woman. In fact, he had a slight paunch that Alma immediately attributed to too many nights enjoying fancy beers in the company of men who shared most of his interests. He would go last. His legs or paunch would do.

The three volunteers walked up to Alma awkwardly. She thought about the plethora of changes people go through the second they realize they're being watched. Then she wondered about the effect of extreme violence on those people.

Alma grabbed them all by the elbows and set them up about three feet apart on the center of the stage, looking toward the audience. Then she pulled back behind them and lifted her empty hand. The lights died. Darkness covered everything. Out in the audience, a few phone screens blinked out as people realized they were now the only source of light.

"Ogún!"

In the dark, silent theater, Alma's scream was a powerful, disembodied thing. She could feel it flying out of her body and entering the ears of those in the audience.

"Ogún is one of the oldest Orishas. He is the owner of kuanagdó, the knife. He is usually depicted wearing his colors, green and black, and sporting a machete or a large knife. He is a fierce warrior who defends his people and fights against injustice wherever he finds it. As every other Orisha, Ogún has many roads. In the Ogún Shibirikí road, he is an angry deity who destroys his enemies. I am his daughter. I follow him on this road. I, too, am driven by bloodlust grown out of my thirst for justice. Luces!"

The lights exploded, momentarily blinding the audience and the volunteers. Behind them, Alma's right hand was held high, the machete reflecting the newborn light.

"Ogún, hear my prayer to you! Oh, vencedor de demandas, tus terrenos lo verde, las plantas y las matas. Acudo a ti para limpiar mi cuerpo, mi mente, mi alma y la de estas personas que comparten este espacio conmigo hoy!"

The machete sliced through the air quicker than lightning. The blade, propelled by every ounce of Alma's

169

strength, anger, and newfound devotion, flashed for a moment and sunk into the plump man's flesh, in the space between his head and shoulder. A guttural scream escaped his throat. Instead of lifting, Alma pulled on the blade and felt it slice through soft flesh and tendon with ease, scraping bone in the process. The man's shoulder shifted a bit, as if he was looking at himself in different side-by-side mirrors. She lifted the bloody tool and brought it down again, this time on the back of the man's head. The machete bit into his skull with a loud crack that shot down the machete and hurt Alma's elbow. The scream died like a TV turning off. The man dropped, almost yanking the blade from Alma's hand. She looked up the second the body hit the floor. Everyone was still sitting. They looked uncomfortable, but she could see some of them thought it was all part of her performace. Others looked undecided, apprehensive. The pigs' blood had done its job.

"Ogún, haz que quien nos deseó mal se arrepienta, se aleje y se vaya. Haz que quien quiera perjudicarnos se inmovilice para que no pueda hacer nada."

The young woman had turned to look at Alma after the man fell. Their eyes met. Alma saw crippling fear blossom in her eyes. She was going to run. Alma grabbed the machete with both hands and swung it like a bat at the woman's left arm. She expected it to cut to the bone. It didn't. Instead, the blade cut through it and bit into her side, stopping only after it had embedded about an inch of unyielding metal into her soft, accommodating flesh. The arm dropped to the floor with a thud. Someone in the first row gasped. Screams flew over the audience like angry birds. The woman looked down in shock. Her body trembled like a kid with an awful fever. Her eyes rolled back. The fall was majestic; a perfect arc of blood shooting into the air like a sacrifice. Alma looked down at her, at the blood squirting from the place where her arm had been, and smiled.

This was it. This was beautiful chaos. This was her rebirth in the mouth of death. This was her dance with Ogún. This was blood quenching the thirst for vengeance that had invaded her recently. This was the strange attractiveness of her ghastly visions come to life in an explosion of arterial red. This was just the beginning of her retribution.

Heavy steps brought her back from her celebratory reverie. The young man was moving toward the stairs backwards. His eyes looked like they were going to pop out of his skull. He screamed something unintelligible. A threat. Someone responded from the audience, told him to run. Alma looked down. There was a lot of movement. Screams. The nervous buzzing of angry bees reached her. It was time to go to work.

"Ogún, te pido que me des salud y que quites de mi camino la maldad. Dame tu mano poderosa para poder vencer todas las batallas que me tiendan."

She took two quick steps and lunged at the man, the machete like a spearhead in front of her.

"Préstame tú escudo para cubrirme de la falsedad y de la hipocresía del mundo. Protégeme de la maldad y no me abandones en la batalla que tengo en este momento."

The machete entered the young man's midsection as he was starting to turn around. Alma felt the metal slicing through his innards in her wrist and elbow, a slight resistance that felt satisfying. She pulled the machete out and lashed out with it again in a wild sideways arc. It caught the man's forearm, which he had brought forward in a silly attempt to protect himself. The flesh in his forearm pulled at the machete like a child refusing to let his mother go. Then it opened like a smile and revealed a pink and white interior that quickly filled with blood. Alma swung again, aiming for his face. The machete bounced off his forehead and slid down the right side of his face, taking his glasses and a chunk of flesh with it. The man dropped. The sounds coming from his mouth reminded Alma of a dog she'd once seen when she was a young girl. A car had run over its back legs, and the animal was dragging itself across the street, howling something akin to the death of a thousand planets. Alma stood above the man, who was cradling his face as he howled, and lifted the blade with both hands before bringing it down on the writhing figure. The top of his skull caved in like a cracked egg. It took two pulls to yank the tool out.

The screams were everywhere now, a cacophony of fear. People pushed at each other, trying to clear the seats, which stood their ground like silent sentinels. People yelled desperately into cell phones, trying to explain something they didn't understand. Others had made it to the door and were pummeling it with hands and feet. Alma jumped from the stage onto the first row.

"Ogún, con tu espada de plata protégeme y defiéndeme de todos mis enemigos. Yo confió en ti y en tu protección y por eso te entregó mis enemigos, que son todos en este maldito teatro. Te entregó sus pensamientos y su sangre para que no tengan poder sobre mi. Te entrego su maldad y su racismo para que no me dañen ni a mi ni a nadie más."

As she prayed, Alma walked forward and swung the machete as hard and as fast as she could at anything that moved. People fell down and tried to climb over each other, their humanity reduced to pathetic screams and a primal instinct of survival that brought forth every animalistic instinct in their bodies.

"Ogún, levanta tu espada y véncelos por el poder que tienes de vencer. Porque eres guerrero de bravura, de estirpe y valentía."

A woman tried to tackle Alma from the left. She turned just in time and buried the blade into her oncoming form with both hands. The woman howled and dropped, her falling body snatching the machete from Alma as she went down. Alma reached down and pulled out the one dangling from her hip.

"Ogún, no permitas que ejércitos o legiones del mal dobleguen, perjudiquen o maleficien mi siembra, cosecha, herramientas, mi casa, ni absolutamente nada."

Warmth filled Alma's chest. She was ecstatic. The coppery taste of blood in her mouth alerted her to the fact that she was laughing as she slashed. With every pull of the machete, blood rained down on her.

This was the festival of sacrifice she'd been yearning for. This was the death of racism in the name of a dark-skinned god. This was the lesson entitled people would talk about for years. This was the celebration of justice all oppressors and colonizers deserved. This was…

"Alma! Stop!"

She turned. Mr. Wilson stood about six feet behind her. In his meaty white hands, a black gun shook like a leaf in the wind. The tiny black hole of its barrel promised oblivion. Alma's smile withered on her lips.

"Don't fucking move! I will…"

She raised her hand. She was going to throw the machete at him and keep dishing out justice. The thing driving her demanded more blood, more righteous punishment.

The orange explosion registered in Alma's brain a fraction of a second before the sound. A muzzle flash. She knew what had happened, but refused to believe it. This was her time. This was the performance of her lifetime.

The warmth inside her chest fizzled out and was replaced by pain. Deep, unbelievable pain. Alma tried to breathe, but her lungs refused to work. The world shifted and her knees hit the floor with a crack. The warmth was back, pouring out of the hole in her chest and caressing her body on its way down.

Alma touched her chest through the soaked shirt. Mr. Wilson was screaming at her. An apology. She looked up. There were tears running down his face. The screams were pushing down on her, shoving shadows into the corners of her eyes.

In the distance, sirens screeched. Their distinct sound flew over that of the people. Someone kicked Alma from behind. The floor flew up to meet her face. Teeth cracked. Her body twitched. Her ears shut off the mayhem. She hoped this level of revenge was enough to go viral.

Nothingness engulfed her affectionately, indiscriminately, elatedly.

LA BRUJA

Resolve was a fickle beast. Vengeance was a capricious lover. Anger was a planet covered in water that simultaneously obeyed the pull of too many whimsical moons. Pain was an unstable variable in a secret equation written in a language that never existed. Confidence was a fragile thing dangling over a sea of crushing teeth by a thread of shadow tied to a beam of hope.

Inmaculada floated across the desert, soaking up the energy of all living things she encountered. She felt the pull of respite almost as much as the need for retaliation. The conflicting emotions confused her. How much blood was enough? How long should she stay on this plane while her family waited for her on the other side? What was her energy doing?

This last question came and went. It crashed into her with the power of a scared bull and then ebbed as the fire inside her obliterated her concerns. The only thing she knew was that events were happening. She felt the power of blood spilled in her name, in the name of holy justice. But she also detected severed connections. She didn't know the people who drank her words from the wind, but she sensed them out there like ghost limbs reaching out to her as they did her bidding. She also sensed when they ceased to be. The connection dropped, like a phone call on a rainy day. The ghost limbs simply vanished. Part of her knew what that meant, but a stronger part of her repeated that loss is always a part of justice, that death is an inevitable conclusion of consecrated reckonings.

Inmaculada listened to the wind, the coyotes howling, barking, and yipping their song in the distance, the rustle of small critters scrambling to stay alive in the inhospitable land around her. She detected the electricity of life everywhere, the songs of spirits satisfied with their current state, the angry cries of those tethered to something they couldn't control. She stopped moving and soaked it all in. The wind carried the echoes of old tears spilled for those who had passed on. It carried the sound of drums made to sing for gods that predated everything humanity thinks it knows. It carried the debris of shattered souls, lost prayers, childhood dreams abandoned under the weight of reality.

When fury diminishes, the space it used to occupy is filled by sorrow or dissatisfaction, or it remains empty, like an abandoned house ready to be invaded by vermin. This was the thought occupying Inmaculada's soul. She wanted to maintain a strong grasp on her odium, but sadness threatened to weaken her grip. She wanted to remain a destructive force, but she missed her son too much. She was tired. She was still livid, but she was exhausted and wanted nothing more than to be near her son again, to allow his energy to fill her with joy.

PEDRITO

Pedrito had asked for milicianos and that was exactly what Santos was going to give him. In fact, he was going to give him more than that. According to the man's explanation, the house they were going to go into was full of "putos animales" who trafficked kids caught on the other side of the border.

"Estos pinches cabrones have no moral compass, mijo. They only care about money. This is my frontera. I am the king of death in this place. I support every fucking dirty business going on around here. I've been helping los carteles get rid of their bodies for as long as I can remember, but dealing with kids is bad for business. It's bad for the soul. Innocence is untouchable, you hear me? Traficar niños es algo que ni el propio Chamuco haría. Kids are blameless, me entiendes? Además, having all that going on around here is bad for all other businesses. That's why we're here. I don't want fucking drones going over my house looking for these pinches mocosos. You and me will send a message. I knew you were a special present from Santa Muerte after you killed my man. A sign. I obey Santa Muerte, and I heard her loud and clear. Once we're done with those cabrones, people on both sides of la frontera will know that fucking with kids will not be tolerated."

The speech had come before the instructions. Pedrito was ready for a plan, but what he got didn't amount to one. Santos said they were going to walk to the front door together and knock. Santos was going to pretend he was trying to sell Pedrito. Everyone knew him. He was the king of death. He was the stewmaker. He was a bad man in their eyes, so no one would think anything of him showing up and trying to make some money off a stupid kid. Once inside, when everyone relaxed a bit, he would pull out his Uzi and Pedrito would pull out the gun Santos had given him, the same he had used back at the house. Basically, the way Pedrito understood it, they were going to walk in and kill everyone who wasn't a kid, every person who was not in a cage. Then they'd set the kids loose and call someone to come pick them up.

Pedrito wanted to see himself in there. He wanted to see himself dishing out justice. However, the images were not in his head. The movie had stopped. His mind was empty. He couldn't see beyond this moment, about 200 feet from the house, sitting in the dark with Santos. The present was everything. The darkness ahead scared him.

THE MOTHER

The Boy slept. The house creaked and groaned. The night went on outside like all things that don't depend on people: unstopping, uncaring, absolute. The Mother trembled. She couldn't feel her legs. The fingers holding the knife communicated with her brain intermittently. Her tongue, now the sole inhabitant of her mouth, rummaged around like a lost dog near a dumpster.

The plan was easy: wait for the monster to come out and cut it to pieces, then burn those pieces in the sink and allow water to take them far away from her home. Execution, however, was a different story. Her joints were almost immobile, as if they'd been welded together. Every movement ripped a crack from them. Every step she took was an agonizing lifetime in a world made solely of pain. She felt slow and defeated.

The fingers twitched. She remembered the knife. She strained to hear the Boy's breathing. It was there. Such a simple sound, but also a miracle and a salve and all the encouragement she needed.

Time was imperceptible because every second was an eternity. Minutes blurred into visions of dead children in their cribs, their parents howling their loss over their torn bodies. Hours went by.

Finally, the stirring began. Movement and bubbling reminiscent of indigestion. Pressure. Dilation. Opening.

The thing was outside. Its body made the thin mattress shift under the Mother's legs. Then a wet plop and the vanishing of that pressure, the cessation of all movement.

The Mother gave it everything she had and managed to sit up. The creature was near the door now, undoubtedly ready to head out for another night of unholy feasting.

The Mother placed her hands on the mattress, the right one a fist pregnant with death, and moved back and forth a few times. Momentum helped her get to her feet.

Pain exploded in her knees. Her lower back felt like half a dozen knitting needles had been shoved into it at once. She moved. Right foot up, down. Pain. Left foot up, down. Agony.

The Mother repeated the process. She listened to the Boy breathing throughout. The thing by the door had stopped moving. Its eyeless face was tilted up, pointing in her direction. She moved faster, ignoring the pain, ignoring the warm, salty tears running down her face.

She was close. One more step. The creature remained motionless. Then a darker line opened in its head. A mouth. It was lined with tiny teeth.

"Mamá."

The word almost knocked her down. Instead, she allowed her body to fall forward, her right hand driving the knife into the top of the thing's head. There was a loud crunch. The blade sunk into soft flesh. The creature squealed like a stabbed piglet. Tiny hands wrapped around the Mother's hands. Feeling them on her skin was so disgusting it threatened to tear consciousness from her and throw her down a well she knew she'd never leave. Instead of passing out, she moved sideways, yanked the knife from the squirming body, and drove it down again. The squealing went up, became a wet, throaty sound, and then stopped. The monster wasn't moving. The Mother kept stabbing. She swung the knife up and down until the body of the creature that had been invading her womb was a pulpy red and grey mess. She kept swinging the knife until the creepy hands were unrecognizable. With each move-ment, her body felt a tad more limber. Energy crept back into her. She sped up. Something vicious inside her had been unleashed, and she relished the sensation.

A few minutes later, minutes that had felt like something without a name that existed beyond time, the Mother stopped moving. Her lungs expanded greedily. She placed her hands on the floor and slipped on the gory mess around her.

The knife clattered on the floor when she dropped it. Her knees didn't scream as she placed them underneath her body and pushed herself up, feeling at least a hundred pounds lighter.

She was covered in a slimy substance, dark blood, and bits of gray flesh, but she moved toward the Boy anyway. The Mother looked at him until his form blurred from the tears in her eyes. She kneeled down next to his small bed and hugged him. The Boy grunted, pulled closer to her, and kept sleeping. In that wonderful, empty silence, she said, "Te amo, hijo." She said it again. Then she said it one more time. She kept repeating it until the sun came through the windows, its light as huge, powerful, warm, and all-encompassing as her love.

THE COYOTE

The coyote grabbed his gun, placed it on top of the wheel, and rested his forehead on top of his hand. Then he closed his eyes and prayed.

"Sagrada y venerada Virgen María, Madre del Padre Eterno, Madre de nosotros también, pura y celestial, consagrada y siempre fiel al Redentor, tu amor es infinito y tu humildad es eterna, tu misericordia y tu andar son la prueba más grande de tu fe.

"María de Nazaret, tú nos cautivas y haces más grande nuestra fe, nos adoptaste como hijos, nos acoges bajo tu manto, nos defiendes y nos proteges, no permitas que la maldad se nos acerque, intercedes por nosotros ante Dios, y con la más firme convicción, ruegas y pides por nosotros.

"¡Oh Madre y salvadora nuestra quien acepto llevar a Jesús nuestro maestro dentro de su vientre, quien sufrió al ver en una cruz al Altísimo, quien con fervorosa oración y en constante alabanza, vive y permanece en el Reino de los Cielos y desde allí nos acompaña.

"Madre mía y del mundo entero, hoy veneramos tu nombre santo, hoy te agradecemos por tu ayuda incondicional, oor ser corredentora del mundo, por ser la más fiel y entregada mujer, ejemplo para todas acá en la tierra, pura y casta sin igual.

"Te pido que me sumerjas en tu miel angelical, que me tomes en tus manos, que tu manto me proteja y que goce de tu presencia. Amén."

With the prayer done, there was nothing left to do except go into the house and do what he'd come to do.

The house looked abandoned except for the lights inside, which the coyote could see break the night as conspicuously as splatters of blood on a white wall.

He didn't want to look suspicious, so he decided to drive his truck almost to the front door and simply knock on it. As he approached, driving around it, the front of the place came into view. A man was standing at the threshold. He was holding a kid by the shoulders as he talked to another man, who was holding a large rifle in his right hand. The man lowered his weapon, nodded, and stepped aside. The man moved, pushing the kid with him into the house.

The coyote was going to have to be incredibly fast and accurate, but he knew that all things were possible with the Virgencita on his side. He was her holy warrior. He was her sanctified arbiter and executioner.

He parked about ten feet from the door on a gravel pathway and looked once again at the gun in his hand. He reverently brought it up to his face, opened his hand, and kissed the image of the Virgencita on the grip. After the kiss, he replaced the gun in the back of his pants, killed the engine, and stepped out into the hot air of the desert.

As he approached the door, he wondered how many men were inside the house. He had a second gun in his pants, a 9mm Padre Frank had let him borrow. That thing had 17 rounds in its black belly. Between the two guns, he trusted he had enough bullets to get the job done.

The coyote took a deep breath and knocked on the door. A few seconds passed. He could see light in the peep-hole. Something cut that light off. A moment later, the door opened. A man stood there, rifle ready.

"Who are you and what do you want?"

He had his lie ready. Excitement flooded his body as he said the words, especially the name he'd picked for the occasion.

"My name is Salvador. I run a little party service for gringos who like them young. I hear you guys have some fresh blood coming back from the other side. I'm just here to talk business and look at the merchandise."

The coyote expected the man to put his hands on him to check for weapons, but he did no such thing. Instead, he lowered the rifle and signaled with his head for him to enter.

As soon as the coyote entered the house, he stopped, put his back against the wall, and looked at the man as if asking for directions. If the man signaled for him to keep walking straight, things would get complicated. Luckily, he didn't. He was tired, underpaid, a rookie, or a combination of those things. The man pushed past the coyote and walked down a dark hallway toward the light at the end of it, which looked like a well-lit living room with white tiles on the floor. The coyote knew the Virgencita was blurring the man's brain, making him act like an idiot and simplifying the process so he could walk away from this victorious, his divine mission accomplished and his body unscathed.

Voices came from the living room. The coyote knew whoever was in there was engaged and wouldn't pay too much attention to him, because the man who'd come to the door would be in front of him, a shield in many ways. With the entrance to the living room a couple of feet in front of them, the coyote jumped forward as he pulled his gun, wrapped his left arm around the man's throat, and placed the gun against his head.

A gun erupted. A spray of shots. Some sort of machine gun. The coyote stopped moving forward, frozen in place by fear and surprise. One second of silence. A second spray of bullets came, followed by a scream. Two loud pops from a different gun joined the cacophony. The coyote pushed forward.

Two men. One tall, one short. Guns in their hands. The coyote moved his arm, aimed. The first man went down. A small submachine gun rattled as it hit the tiles. He moved the gun six inches to the left, squeezed the trigger. The short man moved back, dropped his gun. The coyote squeezed the trigger again. The small man crumpled. The gun flew back to the man he was holding. He pushed his head back as he squeezed the trigger again. The man's skull blew open on the opposite side. The body hit the wall and fell forward.

The coyote looked at the living room. There were four bodies on the floor besides the two he had added. Blood was pooling around them, covering the white tiles like a small flood.

Seven bodies total. He didn't understand. What had he walked into? He stepped into the living room, stood still. No movement. No sounds of ragged breathing. No whimpering. Death's silent hand covered everything. The coyote kept his gun in hand, finger on the trigger. He took a couple of steps forward, closer to the two bodies nearest to him, the two he had shot.

The first one looked like a homeless man. His dark skin glistened. The open mouth revealed teeth ravaged by bad hygiene. White eyes looked up at nothing. They'd never blink again, and the coyote smiled.

The second body was on its side. The coyote walked over to it, pushed at its shoulder with his boot to look at his face. The short man was not a man. No beard. No lines on his face. The coyote looked at the shoes. Small. The shirt. Too fucking small. No veins in his forearms. No visible tattoos or scars. It was not a short man. It was too small, too thin, too delicate. It was a fucking kid. He'd shot a kid. He had killed a kid.

A kid.

He killed a kid.

His mind stopped working. His lungs refused to expand. His heart jumped to his ears. All the coyote could hear was his own pulse. In his head, two words:

A kid.

A kid.

A kid.

He'd seen the gun in his hand. It was there, about a foot away from his right hand. The kid had had a gun. He shot him thinking he was a man. It was okay.

Except it wasn't. He was the savior. He was here to make things right. His entire adult life had been about helping kids, and now he had killed one.

He brought his gun up and placed it under his chin. It was still hot.

Then he remembered the grip. He brought the gun up, opened his hand, and looked at la Virgencita. She was smiling at him. The smile was her approval, her blessing, her command to go on and keep doing his righteous work.

The coyote stood next to the body of the kid, tears of joy falling from his eyes. He opened his hands to the sky as a thank you. He had to find the children and save them. He had to finish his holy mission. But first he would stand there, surrounded by evil men now dead, and pray for a minute as salty tears invaded his mouth through the smile that parted his lips.

LA BRUJA

No beginning is ever assured. No end is predictable. Only the terrified cloak their fragile minds and spirits in a comfortable layer of certainty.

Convictions waver. Absolutes dissolve into vagueness as fury subsides, as passion drowns in repetition, as knowledge is gained, as bigger things begin to dwarf what we once thought of as monolithic beliefs.

Inmaculada was as much a victim of bad people as she was a victim of herself. The anger in her being had spoiled a good heart, damaged a soul full of light, transformed her into an entity full of things diametrically opposed to the caring gentleness that had defined her as a mother, wife, daughter, friend, and curandera.

The magic words she had let loose in the air had done their job, but the cost of it was now reaching her, flooding her with dark feelings and a new kind of pain. Regret was like a remora. Her rage had turned into poison.

The ties that had been severed were now many. She felt the space between her state and the next one filling up with the screams of angry ghosts. Justice had been revealed to her as a shifting, slithering beast killing her all over again. Subjectivity had crept into her system like a pack of rats and gnawed at her for days and nights.

Inmaculada had achieved something, but she wasn't clear on what exactly that something was. Death. Mayhem. Anger. Sacrifices. Blood in the name of her son. Those felt great. The coyotes howled a celebration for all of it. The earth buzzed with the energy it drew from drinking the blood of evil people. But there was also a sadness. A shattered innocence. An echo of her dead son was coming to her in the wind. Blood she didn't want on the ground soured the outcome. It was like the wind was made of knives, cutting into her, blaming her for a loss that equaled her own.

Inmaculada screamed into the night. Her cry, charged with pain and loathing from the moment she had become this new thing, now also carried with it a toxic amount of remorse and despondency. Knowing whether or not her job was done was impossible. Changing everything was impossible. Destruction was part of the answer and certainly something many deserved, but it wasn't the only element necessary for change.

She understood that happy endings, bloody or not, belonged to the realm of fairytales.

The pull of her son was getting stronger as the truth of her actions muddled her conviction. Sticking around the desert stopped making sense as abruptly as it had started to look like the only feasible option. Inmaculada felt trapped between two interstitial spaces.

A memory came as the last invisible feathers from her last cry vanished into the cracks in the ground. Her son, smiling, his tiny arms reaching for her. His smell, a miracle that hung in the air, constantly reminding Inmaculada it would disappear forever as her son transitioned into a toddler. The heavy warmth of her wrapped child in her arms, his clumsy fingers swatting air as they reached for her hair. The smile in his toothless mouth more powerful than anything known to man.

Inmaculada knew then it was time. Every end is guaranteed. Nada dura para siempre, excepto las cosas del más allá.

The invisible body she had been occupying fizzled. Inmaculada felt herself disintegrate into a billion particles of energy. Her consciousness flew up, leaving behind the interstitial spaces. There was only one more step to take, one last thing to do before the current end signaled the start of a new beginning. Inmaculada looked at the black space in front of her, smiled at the memory of her son's smile, and moved into a welcoming oblivion she knew held things more important than eternity.

ACKNOWLEDGMENTS

This is my second novel with Broken River Books, and I know it won't be the last. Thank you for giving me a chance then and doing it again now, JDO.

To Cameron Pierce for the seed that became the first chapter of Pedrito's story. To Brian Allen Carr for showing me that a mosaic novel and pulp can coexist.

To the two mentors who were there from day one: Brian Keene and Jeremy Robert Johnson. To Matthew Revert and Paul Tremblay.

Gabi, eres todo.

Juan. Te llevo, cabrón. Siempre.

There are also a lot of people/writers/friends who make the hustle better with their own hustle, love, humor, and presence (online and in the real world). Much love to these folks: Ben Whitmer, David Joy, Stephanie Ocasio, Isaac

Kirkman, Nik Korpon, David James Keaton, Rios de la Luz, Danny Gardner, Renee Pickup, Bracken Macleod, Rob Hart, Todd Robinson, Stephen Graham Jones, Tiffany Scandal, Nate Southard, Lee Thomas, Bram Riddlebarger, Wrath James White, Stephen Kozeniewski, David S. Atkinson, Leza Cantoral, D. Foy, Liam Sweeny, Paul Michael Anderson, Gonzalo Baeza, Jennifer Hillier, John Edward Lawson, Adam Cesare, David W. Barbee, John F.D. Taff, Angel Colón, Anthony Treviño, John Skipp, Jordan Harper, Ben Tanzer, Sam W. Anderson, Beverly Bambury, Jedidiah Ayres, Bobby Hilliard, Christoph Paul, Shane Douglas Keene, David Nemeth, Brian Evenson, David Bowles, Bud Smith, Carlton Mellick III, Rose O'Keefe, Kelby Losack, Scott Nicolay, Chris Campanioni, Tom Darin, Josh Malerman, Christa Faust, Dan Malmon, Derek Austin Johnson, Jerry Bloomfield, Mike Walker, Terri Lynn Coop, John Hornor Jacobs, Steve Pattee, John Langan, Jose Rodriguez, Dominic Albanese, Tim Hennessy, Matt Serafini, Emma Johnson, Glenn G. Gray, Hector Acosta, Michelle Garza, Tobias Carroll, Adam Howe, Michael Allen Rose, Hugo Camacho Cabeza, Seb Doubinsky, Paul J. Garth, Izzy Lee, William Boyle, Tom Pitts, Ryan W. Bradley, James Ray Tuck Jr, Jason Pinter, John Madera, Steve Weddle, Kent Gowran, Jon Bassoff, Karl Fischer, Ted E. Grau, Laura

Lee Bahr, Leah Rhyne, Linda D. Addison, Matt Coleman, Mary SanGiovanni, Max Booth III, Michael Louis Dixon, Mike Griffin, Nick Mamatas, Noah Cicero, Owen Price, Ryan Harding, Sauda Namir, Scott Adlerberg, John Vercher, Joshua Chaplinsky, and Jose Angel de Dios García.

A la Otredad. A las fronteras. A los exiliados.

Lastly, thank you to books and music for keeping me alive and thank you, reader, for letting me do my thing.

Gabino Iglesias is a writer, editor, professor, and book reviewer living in Austin, TX. His novel, *Zero Saints*, was nominated to the Wonderland Book Award, optioned for film, and translated into Spanish and published in Spain. His words have appeared in publications like *the New York Times, the Los Angeles Times, NPR, the Los Angeles Review of Books, Vol. 1 Brooklyn, HorrorTalk, Criminal Element, The Brooklyn Rail, Heavy Feather Review, Crimespree Magazine, PANK Magazine, The Collagist,* and many others. He is the book reviews editor for *PANK Magazine,* the TV/film editor at *Entropy Magazine,* and a columnist for *LitReactor* and *CLASH Media.* You can find him on Twitter at @Gabino_Iglesias.

For more information on Broken River Books,

please visit:

brokenriverbooks.com

Twitter:

@brbjdo

61806484R00128

Made in the USA
Middletown, DE
20 August 2019